MW01632492

The DECLARATION

Evan F. Nappen and Louis P. Nappen

GUN WRITES PRESS, INC. USA

The DECLARATION

First published in the United States under the title THE DECLARATION by Evan Feit Nappen & Louis Phillip Nappen

Gun Writes Press, Inc.
P.O. Box 12
Oakhurst, NJ 07755
(732) 389-9798

Library of Congress Catalog Card Number: 99-94232

ISBN 0-9670660-1-8

SAN: 299-8971

Registered with the Writers Guild of America, west, Inc.

All characters in this book have no existence outside the imagination of the authors and have no relation whatsoever to anyone bearing the same name or names. They are not even distantly inspired by any individual known or unknown to the authors, and all incidents are pure invention.

The book uses Times New Roman font for main text and drop caps, Impact for chapter titles, Trebuchet for headers, and Courier for newspaper articles.

Cover art by Connie Cabrina Soldi.

The DECLARATION

Dedication

To our parents Barbara and Enoch, who nurtured our individual passions for literature and logic, poetry and politics, art and analysis.

Evan:
To my loving family, my wife Beverly, my sons Ethan and Nathanael, and my American Bulldog Randall. All of whom sacrificed "quality family time" so that this story could be told.

Louis:
To my future loving family, my future wife, my future kids and my future cats.

Acknowledgment

To when liberty and strength of character were encouraged.

CONTENTS

Throughout past history

Liberty has always walked between

the twin terrors of Tyranny and Anarchy.

Theodore Roosevelt
The Great Adventure (1911)

Foundation

a preface by Evan F. Nappen, Esq.

The following is fiction.

Please be advised that I represent Mr. Theodore E. Compass. Attorney/client confidentiality precludes me from either confirming or denying the rumor that I have an actual client who discovered the original Declaration of Independence. There are those, however, who have speculated that this book may be a "trial balloon" floated to judge what to do after such an unprecedented find.

My brother Louis, who is an English teacher, and I prepared *The Declaration* solely on behalf of my client. This is Mr. Compass' story. His views do not necessarily represent those of my brother or of myself.

It is Mr. Compass' intent that the protagonists in *The Declaration* represent three aspects of freedom:

Personal Freedom
Business Freedom
Freedom as a State of Mind.

The antagonists represent three enemies of freedom:

Authoritarianism
Corruption
Elitism.

The incidents occurring after the chapter entitled “We Hold These Truths” is one possible response to the following question:

What would you do if you found
the original Declaration of Independence?

Providence

an introduction by Louis P. Nappen

United States history is replete with ironic, perhaps symbolic, occurrences. For instance —

Presidents Thomas Jefferson and John Adams <u>both died on the Fourth of July</u>, 1826, exactly fifty years to the day after drafting and adopting the Declaration of Independence…

Prior to becoming *General* George Washington, Officer George Washington <u>survived</u> four bullets through his coat and two horses shot out from beneath him during the French and Indian War…

When defender of Constitutional rights, Supreme Court Justice John Marshall, died, the Liberty Bell was tolled in his honor — <u>and it cracked</u>…

Sergeant York, the most honored hero of World War I, was originally drafted <u>as a conscientious objector</u>…

David "Carbine" Williams invented the M1 Carbine, a short-barreled rifle that helped win World War II and the Korean Conflict, <u>while he was jailed on bootlegging charges</u>…

The Declaration of Independence ends with an acknowledgement of our fledgling country's firm belief in "Divine Providence." It should be no surprise that Providence has once again taken a hand in the events that have brought us to this cyclic, historic now.

The two-dollar bill issued in 1976 commemorates the United States of America's Bicentennial. The front honors Thomas Jefferson. The back features an etching based on the painting entitled "The Declaration of Independence" by the Revolutionary War artist John Trumbull.

To Secure These Rights

a brief history

An American shrine.

Continually guarded by armed security and high-tech preservation.

The Declaration of Independence on display at the National Archives in Washington, D.C., is framed in hardened bronze and bulletproof glass with plastic laminate. Ultraviolet-light filters in the laminate give the inner layer a slightly greenish hue. Helium and water vapors are meticulously administered to keep the document fresh.

Every night, the Declaration in its protective case is lowered into a 22-foot tomb made of high-grade concrete and steel weighing over 50 tons. (The vault itself was built by the Mosler Safe Company in 1952, when nuclear bomb shelters were all the rage.) Once the massive top doors of the vault close, the document is preserved from fire, theft, explosion and other threats from man or nature.

A $3,000,000 camera and computerized system continuously monitors the condition of the Declaration. According to the National Archives, the system:

> ...can detect any changes in readability due to ink flaking, off-setting of ink to glass, changes in document dimension, and ink fading. The system is capable of recording in very fine detail one-inch square areas of documents and later retaking the pictures in exactly the same places and under the same conditions of lighting and [reflectivity]. Periods' measurements are compared to the baseline image to determine if changes or deterioration invisible to the human eye have taken place.

When the Declaration first arrived at the National Archives, President Truman said that the revered document "is as safe from destruction as anything that the wit of modern man can devise." For the new millennium, another $4,000,000 will further modernize the encasements. This updated defense will utilize space-age technology of titanium and aluminum to secure the item in an argon environment.

America treasures its founding document.

During the War of 1812, the Declaration of Independence was one of the few papers specifically rescued before the British attacked and burned Washington, D.C.

In 1903, President Theodore Roosevelt directed that the Charters of Freedom, including the Declaration of Independence, be given official custody to the Library of Congress, thereby giving it a new home and the opportunity for permanent exhibition to "the patriotic public."

At the start of World War II, the Declaration of Independence was taken to Fort Knox's bullion depository via railroad guarded by armed

Secret Service agents and a cavalry troop of the Thirteenth Armored Division. For the trek, the document was secured between two sheets of Manila paper and carefully wrapped in a container of all rag, neutral millboard. It was then placed in a specially designed, padlocked, lead-sealed, bronze container which was finally packed in a crate. The entire conveyance weighed approximately 150 pounds.

In 1952, the National Archives officially received the Declaration of Independence with a formal parade down Pennsylvania and Constitution Avenues. The entourage consisted of twelve members of the Armed Forces Special Police, 88 servicewomen, an armored Marine Corps personnel carrier, a color guard, ceremonial troops, the Army Band, the Air Force Drum and Bugle Corps, two light tanks, four servicemen carrying submachine guns, and a motorcycle escort. Both sides of the parade gauntlet were lined with Army, Navy, Coast Guard, Marine, and Air Force personnel.

Currently, it is rumored that a U.S. Airforce jet exists with the primary mission of flying our founding charters to safety in the face of a homesoil enemy attack.

The amount of money, manpower and brainpower applied to the continued protection of the United States' Declaration of Independence exceeds the care given any document in the history of mankind. It is the most guarded manuscript ever known.

However, few people know that the Declaration of Independence on coveted display at the National Archives in Washington, D.C., protected by millions of dollars in high-tech security, is truthfully a third edition of the Declaration of Independence, an engrossed copy on parchment prepared in late July 1776. Actually, some delegates did not sign this document until years after it was published, and a few delegates never signed it at all.

It is a fact of history that the original Declaration of Independence approved by the Continental Congress was lost to the ages.

*

Jefferson recorded in his personal journal that a *fair copy* of his Declaration was made from his handwritten and heavily edited Committee draft. This *fair copy* was the first Declaration of Independence actually approved by Congress. Jefferson wrote that the other members of the Committee of Five set up to draft the Declaration:

> …unanimously pressed on myself alone to undertake the draught [sic]. I consented; I drew it; but before I reported it to the committee I communicated it separately to Dr. Franklin and Mr. Adams requesting their corrections… I then wrote a *fair copy* reported it to the committee, and from them, unaltered to the Congress. *(Emphasis added.)*

Upon approval by the Continental Congress, Jefferson's *fair copy* was delivered to a Philadelphia printer named John Dunlap who published broadside editions, one of which is posted in the Rough Journal of the Continental Congress. Therefore, the later publication of the Declaration of Independence, symbolically signed by members of the Continental Congress and currently on guarded display at the National Archives, is at the very least, a <u>third</u> copy.

The Library of Congress houses Jefferson's Committee draft of the Declaration discovered after his death. As Jefferson noted, Franklin, Adams and the two other members of the Committee of Five hand-wrote numerous, minute and virtually illegible changes to Jefferson's working draft; over eighty changes were made to the four pages. Only Jefferson himself, perhaps, could have deciphered the Committee's final mess. Undeniably, this Committee draft was not the *fair copy* proffered to Congress, adopted, and then given to John Dunlap for mass printing. Also, John Hancock's signature of approval (as President of the Continental Congress) is not on these Committee draft sheets.

For over two hundred years, no living person knew what happened to Jefferson's *fair copy* — the original Declaration of Independence, officially approved by the Continental Congress, signed by the President and Secretary of the Congress, and delivered to Dunlap for printing. Revisionists have attempted to obscure the fact that the original

Declaration of Independence approved by the Continental Congress was lost and not in the possession of the United States Government.

Periodically, the news reports individuals finding copies of the Declaration of Independence. These are simply John Dunlap's second printing or other editions published during or after the American Revolution. Nonetheless, even such early printing-press broadsides auction for enormous sums.

Future Security

Philadelphia, 1776

Three objects reflected the candlelight: a glass tube, a rifle, and a pair of intent eyes. At the far end of the room, a wooden door creaked open. Though the candlelight flickered, the intent eyes never turned from their task.

"Storm's brewing," informed the boy at the door.

"Yes, I know," said John Dunlap, wiping some sawdust and wood chips off the tabletop. "Once you've put the logs down, son, I've something important to show to you... Keep the fire low, just enough to warm up some stew."

The boy rolled his armful of split logs beside the fireplace. After digging the end of a small log into the dying coals, he moved towards the table. "Yes, sir?"

"Remember that hurried article we just had delivered?"

"Yes."

Dunlap waved four sheets of parchment. "Well, here it is: Mr. Hancock's death warrant. This is a declaration of independence from King George, who's going to demand the signers' heads. And probably my own, as well."

He lay the papers back to the table.

The fire crackled.

Dunlap next raised the flintlock off the table. The initials "J.D." were carefully chiseled onto the rifle's stock. Dunlap pointed to where the buttplate had been removed. "Look at the hole I've drilled deep into the wood."

"Won't that weaken the rifle?"

"This gun is made of fine hardwood and shouldn't be affected." Dunlap ran his ink-stained fingers through his white hair. "But, I'm no bloody gunsmith and I did this with haste."

"Why?"

"You know I'm not given to exaggeration. This may perhaps turn as the most vital of all things I will ever tell and show you... Possessing and pressing this declaration is *our* death warrant. I can always deny that the broadsides came from my shop, but if they catch us with the original—"

"Throw it on the fire. We have no need for it anymore."

"This dangerous parchment is proof of our independence from tyranny… I have another idea for so powerful a statement."

He tenderly folded and rolled the four pages of handwritten text into one firm scroll. Then he slipped the scroll into the hand-blown glass tube lying before him on the table. With care, he wedged a glass stopper into the tube and dripped sealing wax to perfect the bond along the edge where glass met glass. Lastly, he slid the full capsule into the rifle stock and again poured wax, flush to the end of the buttstock.

He reattached the buttplate to the stock, concealing the wax-plugged hole, and blew out the flame. Neither man nor boy broke the silence until the thin line of candle smoke disappeared.

Dunlap handed over the rifle. "Now, set this back above the mantle."

The small log the boy had placed on the fire was now fully aflame and lighted the way.

The boy always liked the weight and balance of the flintlock. He liked the rifle even more now knowing that concealed inside was an affirmation for which he and his countrymen were risking their lives and fortunes.

The boy cradled the flintlock before the firelight so that the walnut and steel glowed. He mounted the stock to his shoulder and aimed down the barrel. It was a pleasing fit and he smiled.

Simulating powerful recoils, he rehearsed firing a few rounds.

Delicately, he returned the gun to the deer-hoof rack fashioned years earlier from a buck taken with the very rifle.

With a creaking swing, Dunlap's dinner pot suspended over the live coals.

Immediately, the boy wanted to take the flintlock down again and roll its weight in his hands one more time. But he had chores to finish. Besides, he knew the rifle would be his someday.

Disposed to Suffer

Contemporary America

Storm clouds descended ahead of Ben Vernon's truck with the sweeping motion of an ink smear. In the passenger seat, Ted Compass leaned an open palm out the window.

"Rain."

"Show's held indoors. Don't matter," answered Ben from the driver's seat.

Ted pointed straight up, encouraging, "Some white clouds still above us, though."

"Don't matter…" repeated the older Ben. "White clouds, gray clouds, they'll be there, rain or shine."

"Rain or shine, it sure is nice just to be out of the office," sighed Ted leaning on the door. A steady breeze lashed his dark amber hair against his brow.

"Aren't you close to straightening out that sales tax BS?"

"Yeah…" answered Ted. "But can you believe that I had to — at my own expense — figure out all the materials I purchased out-of-state in order to pay a use tax to New Jersey? It's ridiculous and took a week's worth of man-hours. I'm a civil engineer, not an accountant. And you know, Alice told me there aren't supposed to be any tariffs between states; yet my office and licenses were in jeopardy if I didn't figure it all out and pay up."

"It's legalized extortion. Those money-hungry bastards," sympathized Ben, who tried to refocus the conversation: "Well, this is the fifth year in a row we've made this gun show. Anything particular you're looking for today?"

"Yeah!" Ted's brown eyes sparked. "A nice, representative Rev War piece… And I'll tell you what else: I even want to shoot it."

"The steel in the old days wasn't made to handle modern powders. Just better use a real light charge." After shooting for over forty years, Ben was an expert on guns and loads. "What gave you this bug?"

"Not sure exactly. You know, I've always had a feel for the American Revolution. I'm currently reading a biography of Jefferson, and Alice and I are planning on visiting Colonial Williamsburg again for the anniversary of our first date."

"You should have a decent chance of finding a Rev War flintlock. The threat of rain may keep some people off the highways, but I've never known a little bad weather to keep gun dealers or collectors from doing this show."

Route 78 stretched clear for miles with the sole exception of Ben's truck. White lines filed beside the tires steadily as fingertips down a quill. Every five minutes or so, a car would pass, eastbound, headlights on, attempting to outrace the advancing thunderclouds.

Billy Joel's "Innocent Man" played on the radio, though barely discernable through the wind in Ted's ears. Ted stared at the approaching stormfront just below the bronze tint along the brim of the windshield. An orange outline glowed where the diving sun hid behind the edge of the world. The steady rays reflected in Ted's eyes.

Rain had always been lucky for Ted. He caught the biggest fish of his life with his father during a horrendous downpour. He remembered standing on the front porch with his father beside him holding the trophy bass while his mother took a photo of the two of them. "I don't know who's wetter, you two or the fish," she laughed... He remembered how the first time he met his girlfriend he looked like he had just walked out of a lake. Alice's car was stalled in the rain; however the jumper cables Ben had given him made Ted a momentary hero, and the cup of coffee Ted and Alice shared afterwards began their romance... Ted chuckled as he remembered the previous night's fortune cookie which posed: "The traveler prays for sun, while the farmer prays for rain."

"Damn it!" shouted Ben.

Ted snapped out of his cloud-watching contemplation.

"Damn it!" Ben repeated, tightening down his baseball cap, then double-fisting his steering wheel. Ben's eyes pierced on the rearview mirror. His eyebrows meshed to one solid "V".

Ted tilted his head to scan his sideview mirror. A light blue Caprice grew in perspective. Soon, blinking headlights, a hood and a chrome grill filled the mirror. OBJECTS IN MIRROR MAY APPEAR CLOSER THAN THEY ARE, Ted reread between every other high-beam strobe. Neither man twisted his head fully backwards, guilty-like, to look out the back windshield.

"Damn Triangles." Ben re-upped the visor of his cap.

"Didn't you have your detector on?"

"Cop in Canada confiscated it when I crossed the border on my last fishing trip." Ben's brow remained furrowed as he guided his truck to the shoulder and parked. A red glow pulsed in and out of the cab.

"How fast you going?" Ted whispered.

"Only sixty-five."

Ben leaned over to scavenge his glove compartment. Leaning back, Ted peered into Ben's driver-side mirror. With a sharp flick of his wrist, the state trooper snapped closed his unmarked cruiser door and strode forward evenly — clip-clop, clip-clop — to the side of Ben's vehicle.

"License. Registration. Insurance."

Ben had them ready, and in that order.

"Do you know how fast you were going?" the officer asked.

"Speed limit?" Ben posed.

"No, you were doing seventy."

"I thought the limit was raised."

“Not to seventy. Where you headed?” The officer angled stiffly forward from his waist, forcing his triangular shoulder patch into the window. As it came into view, the yellow patch proclaimed: “N.J. Police State.”

“I asked, ‘Where you headed?’” It appeared as though the officer’s words were coming from the patch and not the person.

“Allentown,” Ben answered.

“Home?”

“No.”

None of your business, Ben thought.

“Hmm?…

“There’s a show…” Ben said. “We’re late for…” he mumbled.

“Now you’re even later.”

The trooper motioned Ben’s papers at Ted. “*Your* license, too.”

“Huh?” *Why?* Ted reluctantly yanked his wallet from his back pocket and rummaged through it. One side held several business cards promoting Ted’s civil engineering services. The other leather pockets held the following:

> Library card, wholesale club card, video rental card, Easy-Pass toll card, Social Security card, movie ticket stub, photo of Ted and his father taken by his mother, two American flag postage stamps, blood donor card, tattered Firearm ID card, gun club ID card, NRA membership card, hunter safety card, voter registration card, expired McDonald’s coupon, three business cards from potential clients, MAC card, Amex card,

Visa Card, AAA card, two gas cards, METRO card, 'smart shopper' card, medical insurance, prescription card, folded photocopy of his birth certificate, vehicle insurance, registration—

Ahh, driver's license!

"Wait in the vehicle while I process these." Clip-clop, clip-clop…

"Why'd he want mine?"

"This state sucks!" Ben exclaimed under his breath. "It ain't like the old days, when cops knew good guys from bad guys and would just give you a warning. No-oh, these guys gotta meet their quotas."

"Look, he's just doing his job."

"Yeah, so were the guards at the concentration camps."

"Oh, please… Don't equate a speeding ticket with the Holocaust."

"No, it's the same principle. Really. You can't just fall back and say, 'I was following orders' or 'It's just a job.' You have to decide as an individual whether you can morally do what your job may require you to do."

"Giving a speeding ticket is not a heavy moral decision."

"Well, you know these guys do seventy-to-ninety miles an hour in the left lane of the highway all the time without their overhead lights on. These Triangles are the world's biggest hypocrites."

"Well, how else are they gonna catch speeders?"

"Think about what you just said, Ted. If speeding is so damn dangerous, why are they speeding up and down the highway to catch speeders?"

"They're trained professionals and they've got a job to do."

"Job? Back to that 'job' nonsense. Truckers, they drive for a living. They could drive fast as safely as cops, but they don't have that option, do they? And they have a job to do." Ben looked back at the trooper in the rearview, then continued, "Does being a police officer mean that you have an elite job? These jobs don't even require college degrees. Instant power-trip. What makes cops better than you or me? I could out-shoot any one of 'em... I was driving before most of them were even born, too. I was driving safely now. There were no other cars on the road, and it hasn't even started to rain yet. Did you feel unsafe? Worried?"

"No… Of course—"

"Then, what's the problem? There was no problem with me. The problem's with the system." Ben's callused hands were two fists squeezing the steering wheel and the corners of his lips were tight. "And try fighting one of these tickets. The courts are completely slanted against the defendant. The towns want to make the money and the insurance companies want an excuse to raise your rates and surcharge you. This is total BS."

Ted had heard such angry lines before from Ben. He sympathized with and understood Ben's frustrations, but wished he'd act a little more adult about getting pulled over. "Remember your blood pressure. Just relax. It happens to everyone."

Ted leaned on his door and studied the crab grass encroaching the asphalt. The grass was curled, desperate for the approaching rain.

"There weren't even other cars on the road!" Ben emphasized again. "And you, as a civil engineer, have explained to me several times how these modern highways can safely handle cars travelling over the posted speed limits. Hell, your father and I helped build these damn roads way back when we worked for Ventura Contracting."

"Honestly, these roads aren't as good as they used to be. Our bridges and infrastructures need work. You don't want to have an accident, do you?"

"The only accident I've ever been in was when that lady backed into me at the post office... No fault insurance. Surcharges. Fines. Points. It's a BS scam. There go my rates."

Ted kept his eyes tilted, downcast, hoping Ben would tirade himself out. A breeze came and rippled the grass in waves like a dry old flag. "What do you want," Ted calmly asked, "to live in the woods?"

"No, here. But unfortunately, it's not realistic because our system is so corrupt. We aren't free. It's a lie; it's a myth. It's like learning that the Tooth Fairy doesn't exist. 'Johnny's gonna grow up to be President.' It was all a lie, a damn, damn lie."

"Don't spout out to me that disillusioned-with-America bull. I don't want to hear it. Not now, at least. It's just a damn speeding ticket. Relax. Look forward to the gun show."

"It's not just a speeding ticket."

The slow clip-clop returned to the Blazer.

At the driver's side window, the officer tore defendant copies from his carbon ticket booklet as if tearing off squares of toilet paper.

"This is for you. Mr. Benjamin L. Vernon, you were speeding."

"And, this is for you, Mr. Theodore E. Compass," said the officer gesturing towards Ted. Ben passed a second beige card from the trooper's hands to Ted's hands. The draft from the approaching card smelled of glove leather and carbon ink. "Mr. Compass, you weren't wearing your safety belt. You're old enough to know better."

Mr. Vernon and Mr. Compass stared at their flimsy tickets with slight hints of disgust. Ted could barely interpret his card's report: a liberal sprinkling of scribbles, stains, streaks and shaded boxes. Ben scanned his summons as best he could, too. Then, turning it over, Ben saw that if he wished to plead *guilty*, he would not have to go to court. *Isn't that cute?* he thought.

"Drive safely. You're heading into a storm."

"Yes, we know," said Ted.

"Have a nice day."

"Thank you, officer," Ben monotoned.

It Is Their Right, It Is Their Duty

Philadelphia, September 1777

"The British have attacked and the Militia has been summoned," said the Minuteman in the doorway of John Dunlap's shop. "Bear your arms and accoutrements and assemble in the town square without delay."

The boy grabbed the printer's flintlock and its possibles bag off the deer hooves and hurried for the center of town. The printer was out buying supplies and would most likely meet him there.

At the town square, however, Dunlap was no where to be seen.

"Get in line, men! We are going to meet the British head on."

Before he knew it, the boy was inducted to help face Cornwalis' column heading into Philadelphia.

To Bear Arms

Contemporary America

Approximately one thousand tables lined the convention hall floor. Each table displayed a specialized array of rifles, shotguns, handguns, bows, knives, militaria, books and pamphlets — all types of imaginable shooting, defense and hunting paraphernalia. There were Colts, Winchesters, Remingtons, Brownings... Lever-actions, pump-actions, bolt-actions... Single shots, double-barrels, repeaters... Breachloaders, muzzleloaders... And every caliber from .17 to .700. The place smelled of old steel and gun oil; it was an affectingly good smell, like that of a new car or a favorite attic. Best of all, this was no museum; if you had the money, you could own any piece of history you found.

"I'll meet you by the front door in three hours. Happy hunting," encouraged Ben rubbing his palms together.

Ted started down the aisles, scanning the tables for Rev War flintlocks. Whenever he spotted a potential candidate, he asked the dealer, "When was this flintlock made?" Most were *post*-Revolutionary War. When Ted did come across an authentic Revolutionary Period flintlock, the dealer always wanted big bucks— five thousand or more.

Throughout the gun show there was a free-market energy. Buyers were in the middle of deals and dealers were in the middle of storytelling about their wares. The aisles were packed and it was difficult to completely scan each table. In fact, the conversations were so constant and the bustling so hectic that Ted forgot there were thunderclouds clapping outside the hall.

Hurriedly, Ben came smiling up to Ted: "My buddy got here late and he was just setting some guns out on his table — He told me that he had a decent Rev War rifle that he would sell reasonably to a friend. I told him to hold it until I could find you. I told him you were seriously interested in picking one up today."

What price was considered reasonable? Stomach tightening in anticipation, Ted gestured his hand outward, encouraging, "Lead the way!"

Life, Liberty

Germantown, October 1777

The boy came to. He did not feel pain, only numbness.

"My rifle, where's my rifle? He'll want it back."

"What rifle? You weren't brought here with any rifle," said the field doctor to the boy recumbent on the ground. "You just relax. Don't worry about any rifles right now. You have got a serious wound, boy. You have got to stay calm."

The boy's white shirt was more red than white. Casualties and groans surrounded him. A smell of a sweat, blood and death lingered.

"I know I downed at least one of them Red Coats. But he's gonna kill me for losing his rifle... an' I was only bringing it for him."

The boy lay there thinking about the rifle and how proudly he and it performed in battle. He remembered how secure he felt with the piece in his arms and the sense of protection that it gave.

He worried about the flintlock's hidden cache as he drifted off. Like a pirate's lost treasure map, the whereabouts and the secret of John Dunlap's rifle was to remain.

Obtained

Contemporary America

Ted knew such a rifle would be his.

He mounted the stock against his shoulder. It was a pleasing fit and he smiled.

This rifle was clearly a battlefield piece. Its condition was fair-to-good, but it was all there. Little finish remained on the metal, but the wood and furniture was tight and strong.

Ted spotted initials carved into the stock. "What's this mean?"

"Who knows? It gives it character," coaxed the dealer.

"Maybe its name is J.D.?" Ben joked. "Anyway, you want to shoot it."

"How'd you get it? Know any of its history?" inquired Ted.

"All I know is, some old lady came into my shop, said her husband died and had this gun. And she 'didn't want any guns in the house.' She went to turn in the gun at one of those crush-and-melt government buy-back programs. Luckily, a customer of mine was in the line and told her that her rifle had antique value and that she should sell it to me for a lot more money than she would get from the cops. — The guy was only there to turn in a bunch of clunkers that he couldn't even give away for parts. But the government paid him fifty bucks apiece to 'get the guns off the street' and make it look like they're doing something about crime. What a joke. With the money, he bought a brand new Colt semi-automatic rifle from me. — Anyway, about your gun. It appears to be a Committee-of-Safety model; it's surcharged 'U.S.' and utilizes a British lock. Such guns were made by local gunsmiths for Committees of Safety."

Ted knew that Committees of Safety were militia-type groups that formed defenses, coordinated supplies, and produced propaganda against the British. Ted hefted the rifle with a sure grip and knew that he was holding a piece of history. There was no doubt in Ted's mind that this rifle was Revolutionary Period.

Again, he raised it face high. The stock's walnut color matched his eyes. The wood felt cool against his cheek and fit comfortably into the flat of his shoulder. *This is just what I've been looking for,* he thought. *I can't wait to fire it!*

The dealer and Ben could tell that Ted and this flintlock were meant for each other.

Always the jokester, Ben feigned to take out his wallet. "If you don't buy it, I will — and give it to you for your birthday."

"Oh, no you don't." Ted lowered the side of the barrel against Ben's forearm. "Cause I couldn't top it."

Cradling the rifle in the crux of his arm, Ted reached for his own thick wallet.

Ben's buddy was obviously giving Ted a break. The price was not only reasonable, it was irresistible.

"Need a gun permit?" Ted queried as he pealed off and counted the cash. "Don't I need to fill out a whole lot of paperwork for this?"

"When you drove over the border, son, didn't you see the sign? You're in Pennsylvania now. 'America starts here.' You don't need to show me or fill out a thing, just like the first guy who ever got this gun over two hundred years ago. This isn't your Garden State... However, I do have to charge you sales tax."

We Hold These Truths

The radar detector shrilled.

Ben immediately pressed the brakes though he was only going 55 miles per hour. As his Chevy tiptoed past a hidden speed-trap, Ben cheered, “Alright! That was a save,” and patted his new radar detector.

“I can’t believe those things are legal.”

“What do you mean, Ted? All it does is let me know if cops are around. Anyway, I can’t afford another ticket, thanks to our trooper friend last week. Besides, a radar detector is just a radio receiver, and the guy at the electronics shop told me that under federal law we have the right to receive any radio signal. However, there is a proposal to ban them, if that makes you happy. Good thing we weren’t pulled over, too, because if the cop had found our guns, we’d have a lot of explaining to do.”

“But we aren’t doing anything illegal.”

“It doesn’t matter whether you’re doing anything illegal or not. In New Jersey, all gun owners are guilty until proven innocent,” Ben explained. “They would still take all our guns and you would never be able to shoot your new flintlock.”

“Are you kidding?”

“No. Remember that guy Frank I barely outshot at the last club match?”

"Yeah, what about him?"

"He was pulled over driving home from the match. They took all his stuff and he still hasn't got it back yet."

"What for?"

"The cops said it was for 'public safety' and that he'd have to get a lawyer to talk to the prosecutor to *maybe* get his property back. The prosecutor is going to file for a forfeiture of his firearms and gun license."

"That doesn't sound right. Are you sure?"

"Absolutely. The Germans did the same thing to the Jews. Only they called it 'expropriation of property.' Frank had some expensive custom pieces, too. And I can just imagine the 'care' being given to them."

The truck turned down a tree-lined dirt road leading to the target range. SUVs, pickups and sedans filled the parking lot. "Wow, the club is busy today," Ben noted. "Hopefully, we can find a fairly secluded spot."

Gravel crunched under the tires as Ben backed into a space by the rifle range. The rifle range consisted of a dirt berm backstop approximately two hundred yards from the firing line. Target holders protruded from the ground at varying distances between the firing line and the berm.

Ted and Ben anxiously carried their gun cases, ammunition and targets from the tailgate to the concrete shooting bench. Faint odors of gun oil and gunsmoke competed with the earthy scent of the autumn woods. Under the covered firing line, a woman announced through a hanging loudspeaker: "The line is now safe." The two friends strode downrange and posted targets. After they and other shooters returned, the line was announced "hot" again.

Ted set his flintlock muzzle up against the concrete bench.

Ted felt confident about muzzleloading. He had fired "smokepoles" many times, but never an authentic piece. He took a three-inch-long plastic tube out of his shirt pocket and removed its cap. In the tube was a prepared measurement of black powder, which he dumped down the bore. Next, he wrapped a grease-coated patch of cloth around a lead ball and placed it over the muzzle until the top of the barrel appeared to have a silk flower on the end of it. He then took a ramrod and pushed the ball and patch down the bore. After ramming the ball all the way, he grabbed the rifle, cocked the hammer, and flipped open the frizzen of the flintlock mechanism.

Earlier that morning, Ted had inserted a new flint in the jaws of the hammer. He now poured a small amount of fine gunpowder into the pan.

His thumb smoothed down the frizzen.

Mounting the gun to his shoulder, he carefully eyed the target.

He gently squeezed the trigger.

The flint-loaded hammer launched and hit the frizzen hard; showering sparks ignited the fine gunpowder in the pan. There was a short "pfffftt" instantaneously followed by a loud bang.

After two silent centuries, the rifle awakened.

Ted let out a hoot: "Oh-yeah! Hit the eight ring, first shot!" Ted inhaled deeply and tasted the white smoke floating around him. He grabbed a jagrod with a patch of cloth hooked on its end and gave the barrel a brisk swab.

"They didn't have the luxury in battle to swab out their bores, ya know," teased Ben.

"I want this rifle to last another two hundred years."

Ted pulled out another powder load and searched the bench for a new patch and ball.

Ben had brought to shoot an original World War II Luger which his father permanently "borrowed" from a Nazi who no longer had any use for it. He was always impressed with the Luger's point-ability. The only problem with the gun was that its mechanism was somewhat complex; Ben's Luger was prone to jamming and today was no exception.

Right after Ted poured his next powder charge down the flintlock's muzzle, Ben shouted: "Damn! My gun stovepiped." The shellcasing of a 9mm parabellum cartridge had lodged in the toggle action as another round started to feed. Ben turned to Ted, "Could you give me a hand with this? I thought I had adjusted the mag-lips to stop this from happening."

Ted nodded and rested his rifle against the bench to give Ben a hand.

"I'm gonna pull the toggle back. You pull the shellcasing out," instructed Ben as he dropped the magazine out of the Luger and pulled. The toggle shifted only slightly, but enough for Ted to pull the shellcasing free. The extra round dropped to the ground.

"Thanks," said Ben.

"Why don't you shoot something more reliable, like a flintlock?" winked Ted, pulling out a handful of yellow tubes with prepared powder charges. "I'm purposefully using standard loads for this ol' girl. Nothin' hot."

Ted popped the cap on another plastic tube and poured it down his barrel.

Ted had just accidentally double-loaded his flintlock.

He took another patched ball, rammed it home, cocked the hammer and charged the pan. Mounting the rifle, he comfortably rested his cheek against the stock. "See that Red Coat out there? He's mine."

Ted pulled the trigger.

The flintlock discharged with a terrible bang. The double charge of Twentieth Century black powder was more than the Eighteenth

Century breech could handle. Bits of wood and metal blew out the side of the rifle.

As Ted fell backwards, the rifle flew out of his hands and slammed hard against the corner of the concrete shooter's bench. Another sharp crack echoed as the rifle's stock splintered in half.

"Oh, my god! Are you okay?!" Ben gasped, pointing at Ted's white shirt which was starting to turn dark blood-red.

Ted immediately lifted his torn shirt. A gash angled across his abdomen. Luckily, the cut was not deep; but it was bleeding.

"Stay there." Ben ran for the first aid kit from the back of his truck. Quickly returning with some sterile cloth and bottled water, he cleaned the surface wound.

Ted still leaned against the bench, visibly shaken. "Where's my rifle?"

Ben commanded, "Don't worry about your damn rifle."

"Please, give me my rifle."

"Okay, okay. Don't move. I'll get it."

Ben walked over to recover the flintlock and stopped short. The breech was blown. His attention was drawn to shards of broken green glass reflecting in the light like drops of rain. The sparkling trail led to a thick, curled parchment protruding from the broken stock.

"Hey, Teddyboy, what the hell is this?" Ben asked as he handed Ted the busted stock with the papers sticking out of it. "A treasure map?... A bill of sale?"

"Hell if I know."

Ted slowly extracted the document from its Colonial sanctuary. He carefully unfolded and leafed through the thick four pages stitched together with a loop of thin red ribbon. His eyes immediately focused on the bottom of the last page which had a giant-sized, fancy signature he immediately recognized as John Hancock's.

"Hey, this must have been John Hancock's rifle!"

Ben pointed at the broken stock. "It has the initials 'J.D.' not 'J.H.'"

Ben knelt down beside his friend. They both started reading the document from the top:

In Congress, July 4, 1776

A Declaration by the Representatives of the United States of America in General Congress Assembled

When in the course of human events it becomes necessary—

"Hey!" Ben realized. "That's the start of the Declaration of Independence! I wonder why it's only signed by Hancock and his secretary, Charles Thomson... Why the hell would that be in your rifle?"

By this time, the firing line had been made safe again. A number of other shooters gathered around to see if they could be of any assistance or if an ambulance was needed. A few bystanders saw the document and were curiously amazed.

"Are you able to get into the truck?" Ben asked.

"Yeah, I'm fine, just a little rattled and scratched. But my rifle is ruined," groaned Ted.

"I'll collect our stuff," said Ben as he eased his friend onto the passenger seat.

Self-Evident

Ben drove directly to Ted's house. After helping Ted out of the truck and through the front door, he aided him onto the living room couch. Ted noticed the answering machine blinking beside him. Ted was expecting a call from Alice, who was working out of state. Instead, an unfamiliar, anxious voice announced:

"Hello, this is Kenny Kent from the *County News*. I heard that you had a newsworthy event at the gun range today. I'll try calling you again."

As soon as the answering machine reset, the phone rang.

Ted picked up the receiver, "Hello, Alice?"

"No, this is Kenny Kent from the *County News*. I called earlier. Is this Theodore Compass?"

"Yes, this is he. What can I do for you?"

"I was told that you found a copy of the Constitution or something like that in your blown-up gun at the shooting range today?"

"Well, it doesn't seem to be the Constitution. It reads like the Declaration of Independence, but it's signed with only two signatures."

"Would you mind if I came by with a history professor and talked with you about it? I've worked with this professor before. He's interested, and he really knows this Americana stuff."

Ted thought to himself, *Well, I really do want to find out about this, why not? But I'm still a little shaken up.* "How about tomorrow?" he asked.

"No, no, the professor won't be around, and I really don't want to wait. You know, deadlines… Come on, what do you say?"

Ted's curiosity got the better of him. "Okay, when do you want to come by?"

"About two hours, okay?"

"Fine," said Ted and hung up the phone.

Ben, who had been attentively listening, said, "Why do you want the media involved in this? You don't even know what you've got yet? Plus, you're still a little shaky from the accident."

"This way we can find out what those papers are. You know I love U.S. history…"

"I don't trust 'em," said Ben. "Some of these newspaper pimps would sell their grandmother for a story."

"This guy sounds over-excited, yet sincere enough. But, Ben, could you stick around?"

"Sure, I wouldn't want to miss your fifteen minutes of fame."

An hour and a half later, the doorbell rang.

"I'm Kenny Kent and this is Professor Leonard Button, Chairman of the History and Political Science Department at the University."

"You're early," noted Ted.

The hyper, skinny Kent strode directly past him and into the house. "Where is it?" Kent demanded. "Pull it out for Dr. Button."

Button appeared to have a genuine interest, but courteously still waited on the welcome mat, reluctant to probe Ted's privacy. The pepper-haired professor sported a reddish-gray mustache, horn-rimmed glasses, and a corduroy jacket with leather elbow patches. Ted invited him inside. Before entering, Button put forward his hand to greet Compass. "Good to meet you. I'm Len Button." Ted felt immediately at ease in the professor's presence.

From a corner chair, Ben skeptically watched the reporter strut around the room. Ted introduced the two visitors to his reticent friend. Ted sat the professor at the living room table and offered them all something cold to drink.

Ben shook his head no.

Dr. Button politely refused, as well.

Kent blurted that he would like a soda.

After giving Kent his glass of soda, Ted pulled out a fireproof safety box. The container held Ted's insurance policies, the deed to his house, his birth certificate, his mother's and father's death certificates, his Selective Service confirmation, his car's certificate of ownership, his passport, some treasured photos, his mother's engagement ring and his grandfather's pocketwatch. Sitting on top of it all were the folded and curled sheets of parchment.

Professor Button removed a pair of white cotton gloves from a jacket pocket and pulled them over his fingers. With great care, he removed and unfolded the document. His eyes immediately lit as he scanned the papers. His breath quickened.

The professor produced a monocle magnifier and inspected the item. Button nodded, then began mumbling: "Pristine paper... Unfaded ink... Punctuation's there... *In*alienable... Jefferson's handwriting... Proper signatures…" Slowly, Dr. Button looked up at Ted and asked, "This was found in the stock of a flintlock rifle?"

"In a glass tube inside a rifle," clarified Ted.

"May I see that rifle, please?"

"What's left of it, sure."

Ben kept an eye on Ted as he went to get the gun.

Swirling the ice in his drink, Kent piped up, "What do you think? What do you think?"

"Just a moment," calmed the professor; "I want to first examine the flintlock." As soon as the broken rifle stock was handed to him, his eyes fixed on the carved initials.

The professor pressed two fingers to his temple and drew in a few purposeful breaths. *It all added up.* He could not believe it; but, incredibly, it was true. Dr. Button spoke, slowly and distinctly: "Mr.

Compass, it appears you have found the original Declaration of Independence which has been lost to the ages for over two hundred years."

Kent forced down his last gulp of soda and saw national bylines.

Ben whispered, "Holy shit."

Ted halted, "Wait a minute. The Declaration is on display in Washington. Every school kid knows that. And it's signed by all the Founding Fathers. What are you talking about?"

Professor Button, pointing at the J.D. on the rifle stock, informed, "The name of the printer who was given the original Declaration of Independence was *J*ohn *D*unlap... Mr. Compass, let me explain. The original Declaration was given to Mr. Dunlap to make a broadside—"

"What's a broadside?" interrupted Kent, who had out his notepad and was scribbling as fast as he could.

"As a newspaper man, Kenneth, you should know that a broadside is a single-sided copy produced by a printer's press."

"You mean," interrupted Kent again, "what that guy discovered when he took apart the picture frame and found an early copy of the Declaration behind the crappy artwork?"

"Yes," acknowledged the professor. "That was a broadside... Back to your query, Mr. Compass. The Declaration on display in the National Archives is actually <u>a third</u> recitation broadside symbolically signed by Colonial representatives over a period of years beginning in

1776. However, what you've discovered here is apparently the original Declaration of Independence, the one officially approved by the Continental Congress before mass publication, written out in Thomas Jefferson's handwriting and signed by the President of the Congress, John Hancock, and attested to by Secretary Charles Thomson."

The professor took out his wallet and removed a two-dollar bill. He laid the bill face down on the table and pointed. "There's Jefferson and the Committee of Five presenting *your* Declaration of Independence to John Hancock for the approval of the Continental Congress."

There was an awed silence.

The professor continued, "That picture memorializes the last time this original Declaration of Independence was seen in public. It is a popular misconception that this picture represents the signing of the U.S. Government's copy on guarded display. But that's simply not true. In fact, Livingston, one of the Committee of Five shown in the etching, refused to later sign the document, believing it was too premature."

Kent questioned, "Well, what's the original Declaration of Independence worth?"

Button glanced to Kent, then to Ted, and replied: "What is the United States of America worth?"

Powers of the Earth

Kent was savvy enough to recognize the impact the publication of this news would have on Ted Compass' life. Nonetheless, he rationalized: The people have the right to know. The story was broken nationally via wire services the following day.

Unfortunately, Ted Compass had a listed phone number.

Six-thirty that morning his phone rang. It was a reporter from a top national newspaper: "Is it true that you have found the original Declaration of Independence?"

Ted's stomach gash pained him for most of the restless night. He did not appreciate this early call, but nonetheless politely yawned, "Yep, that's right."

"Well, tell me: What are you going to do with it?"

Ted rubbed his eyes. The question woke him up a bit more. "Well, I haven't decided yet. What do *you* think I should do with it?"

"I don't make up the stories. I just write 'em."

"Look, I really don't feel like talking right now."

"How much is the thing worth?"

"Look, I really don't want to talk right now."

"Hmmm. May I call back later, then?"

"Fine."

As soon as Ted hung up the phone, it immediately rang again.

A man with a British accent greeted, "Hello, is Mr. Theodore Compass at home?"

"Yes, hello?" Ted responded.

"I am Sir Edwin Gage of the Bartleby Auction House, London Offices. I am calling to inquire as to whether you would like our house to handle the sale of your Declaration."

"Who said I was interested in selling it?" Ted was fully awake now.

"Well, surely you are not considering keeping it? What good would it do you? I am confident that Bartleby would be able to get you tens of millions for this item. Actual governments would most likely bid on it. At the very least, we'd be glad to hold it for you until you have made up your mind."

"Look Mr. Bartleby, if I want to sell it, I'll contact you." As Ted hung up the phone the voice was still talking on the other end.

The phone immediately rang again.

This time it was a different accent on the line. The caller was from some foreign embassy. Ted couldn't make out through the thick inflections whether the man claimed to be from Iraq, Iran or some other Middle-Eastern country. This person, too, questioned the availability of the document.

Ted unplugged the phone jack midcall.

Ted flipped the draped blanket off his legs, checked that the shutters were tightly drawn, and hid the fireproof box with all his valuable documents in his antique grandfather clock. Replugging his phone, he called Ben. While waiting for Ben to pick up, an operator broke onto the line with an emergency phone call from Senator Donald Shears, Washington, D.C.

Ted took the call.

"Is this Mr. Theodore Compass? This is your Senator, Donald Shears. I understand that you have something which belongs to the United States, and on behalf of the United States, I advise that you must return this document. As a United States Senator, I would be glad to make arrangements for you to surrender the Declaration of Independence to Washington. Of course, I would personally assist you, as one of my constituents, in this endeavor."

"Thank you for looking out for me, Senator," deadpanned Ted.

For a third time, Ted hung up on a man still speaking to him.

He again unplugged the jack.

Ted proceeded to his gun safe. The Liberty Safe in his garage was a steel vault approximately the size of a refrigerator. He set the key in the lock and turned the combination dial as he had countless times. Only this time, the safe didn't open. *I can't believe that I messed up the combination.* He focused carefully on manipulating the dial. He counted each turn and stopped precisely on each number. This time the safe smoothly opened with a soft clank.

Out came his custom combat .45 that he used for target shooting. Now, however, he loaded it with jacketed hollowpoints. He also grabbed a twelve-gauge shotgun and loaded it with #1 buck magnum loads; it was reassuring to think that there were twenty .30 balls in each shotshell. As he put the shotgun behind his grandfather clock, there surprisingly came a knock at his back door.

Who the hell is that at this hour of the morning?

Ted slowly opened the door, pistol at his side.

It was Ben. Ted's apprehensive friend scanned left to right, then motioned for Ted to unlock the screen door.

"My phone won't stop ringing," complained Ben as he scrambled into the house. Raising the brim of his cap, he continued, "These idiots are offering me a cut if I could get you to sell. That jerk Kent quoted me as 'the first eyewitness' and 'your best friend.'"

Ted stuck his .45 into his waistband holster.

Ben nodded, "Good choice," and lifted up his own shirt, revealing the grip of his custom .45 as well.

Emigration

"How's that nasty cut healing?"

"Okay. It seems to be healing quickly," said Ted, lifting up his shirt and gently patting the darkening scab.

"I think we should take off for my lake house until this publicity calms down," suggested Ben.

"Good idea, but I have to first call the office and let them know that I won't be coming in. And I have to leave a message for Alice, too."

"Grab your stuff now and we'll use the pay phone around the corner."

Ted removed the fireproof box containing the Declaration and his shotgun behind the grandfather clock.

"I already grabbed my M1 Garand and plenty of .30-06," informed Ben.

"What are you planning on? A war?"

"It wouldn't be the first time the words in that box caused shots to be fired."

Ted threw three boxes of .45 hollowpoints, two boxes of twelve-gauge buckshot and slugs, and a mix of clothing into his hunting pack.

"Don't worry about the small stuff. I've got toothpaste and all up there. Anything else we'll buy."

After loading Ben's Blazer, they took off down the road. At the end of the street, they passed two TV news-vans heading toward Ted's house.

Ben glanced to Ted and reassured, "We'll be at the lake in two hours."

Opinions of Mankind

For ten miles, Ben had been eyeing a dark blue Imperial in his rear view mirror. The sedan finally veered off onto an obscure exit. Ben sighed a little breath of relief.

"Yeah," Ted voiced. "I'm glad to see them turn off, as well."

"God, I'm on edge. Though the .45 in my belt gave me some comfort, I'm not in the mood for any target practice."

"Right. But if we get caught carrying without permits, we're really in trouble."

"Look," briefed Ben. "We've got an item in the back seat that may be worth a billion dollars. Politicians, auction houses, foreign governments, all want it and no stupid anti-gun law is going to stop me from protecting us and what's in that box."

"You're right, of course. That's why I'm cocked and locked, too."

"Let's just put on the radio and try to relax," suggested Ben.

The radio was set for AM talk.

"…Harrison from the Bronx, and I'm sick of all these God-damn drug dealers thinkin' they own the streets. I wanna walk around safe with my kids and my wife, but I worry about dem guys shootin' it out…"

Ben argued at his radio: "It's not the drugs or the guns. It's the money. If drugs weren't worth so damn much, they wouldn't be shooting at each other. You don't see them killing each other over toilet paper, do you? Why do you think everyone wants your Declaration, Ted? Power and money. Remember that. Power and money. Didn't we learn anything from Prohibition? Every anti-drug law we have raises the price of drugs and more people die. Street economics. You'd think these dummies in D.C. would know it."

Ted said, "Well, how come the politicians don't repeal the laws?"

"Because everyone's making money off the war on drugs. Besides the drug lords and corrupt politicians, as long as drugs stay illegal, we need more police, we need more jails, we need more judges, defense attorneys, district attorneys, government-mandated rehab programs, 'feel good' legislation... Why don't we put all this time, effort and money into educating society about the stupidity of irresponsible drug use?"

"I just read that ninety percent of all court cases involve drugs."

"Ninety percent! Could you imagine if all the judicial system had to worry about was *real* crime?"

"But, do you really want kids able to buy and use drugs?"

"No, of course not, Ted. Children have never had the same rights or responsibilities as adults. Drugs can be restricted to children in the same ways that we now restrict children's access to pornography or even to driving a car."

A talk-show host wrapped up his response: "I agree with Harrison. We gotta raise the stakes to show that drug dealing doesn't pay. We need the death penalty for drug-dealers... Next caller."

Diane from Long Island spoke in a nasally voice: "Harrison's just talked about them shooting it out? I feel that guns threaten our children and that their only purpose is to kill. Nobody but soldiers and cops need guns. If a gun ban could save just one person's life, it would be worth it. We need to ban guns."

"She's a stupid bitch," Ben summarized.

The talk-show host replied, "Madam, nobody likes children getting killed. But a gun ban simply won't work. If you ban guns, criminals will still get them and the only people who won't be able to defend themselves are law-abiding citizens."

"Oh," Ben piped. "But banning drugs sure worked. This guy is just conservative party-line. If he really believed his own logic, then he'd believe in freedom across the board."

The talk-show host wrapped up, "That's it for me today, your hosts of hosts, but more talk will be coming at you in just a minute, following a check on today's top stories:

> A sex scandal was alleged during the President's September visit to the Vatican...

> Federal Appeals Court has ruled Boy Scout cleanliness requirement unconstitutional after discrimination against hygienically-challenged homeless teenager...
>
> Original copy of the Declaration of Independence found by New Jerseyan when gun explodes...

These stories, sports and weather at the top of the hour."

"Why don't we turn off the radio," suggested Ted, reaching for the dial.

"Well... We really should stay informed—"

Suddenly the theme from "Mighty Mouse" came over the radio and a new, obnoxious talk-show voice came on: "This is Tori Jane, your liberal guardian. Let's start right off with our first caller, Regina from Jersey City."

"Hi, Tori. Love your show."

"What's on your mind?"

"Last week, you were talking about taxes. I just wanted to tell you how much I agree that we need a more progressive income tax like the one proposed by Senator Shears. It's not fair that some people are rich and some people are poor. As you always say, Tori Jane, it's the Haves vs. the Havenots. We've got to soak the rich. America was founded on the principal that everyone is equal. The only way we're going to solve society's problems is by giving the poor most of what the rich have."

Tori Jane cut in, "What you're suggesting we need is a modern day Robin Hood. I agree."

Ben said, "What a HEAP. In other words, everyone should be equally miserable... I've got an idea. Why don't we start by distributing Tori Jane's wealth?"

Ted asserted, "Do you have a comment for everyone?"

"As a matter of fact, yes. All these political talk-show hosts are so inconsistent."

"Inconsistent about what?"

"Inconsistent about *freedom*," declared Ben. "Those who believe that the government should solve all our problems and dictate what the people can and cannot do are *authoritarian.* Those who believe in freedom are *libertarian.* I've seen this country change. Americans used to turn to themselves and to their communities to solve problems — not only to the government."

"Yeah, I'm starting to see what you mean. It seems like all the government does is make life more difficult for the honest man. At the office, the bureaucrats have imposed so many regulations that I can't hire and fire as I please or buy my supplies from whom I want without paying a penalty. And, my liability insurance is sky high because our civil courts are out of control..."

Ben noted, "Right now, we're breaking the law just because we're attempting to protect ourselves."

For a moment, Ted had actually forgotten why they were on the highway. He craned to check that the safety box was still on the back seat.

Ben continued, "There are so many petty, stupid and intrusive laws that it's impossible to go through a day without breaking one. From how I operate my car to how I decorate my house, there's always some law shaking its finger at me. Hell, remember when Governor Florio banned us from eating runny eggs and taxed our toilet paper?"

"I know what you're saying," agreed Ted. "Individuals should have both rights and responsibilities and not have to be told by or made to ask permission from Big Brother about what they may and may not do or how much money they may make or keep. But what can we as puny citizens do about it?"

"I don't know what we can do about it. Our votes seem lost between the Republican and the Democratic strongholds… You know, I can't even name one positive thing the government has done right for the American people?"

"Well... How about the roads?" offered Ted, pointing down out the windshield.

"The interstate highway system was set in place by Eisenhower on the basis of national defense. The only thing the government has, perhaps, done right is its primary mission: national defense. But they spend a hell of a lot of money doing it and they have made some major blunders. The government needs to return to its primary purpose and gets its fumbling fingers out of all these other areas. Ted, the bottom line is whether or not you believe in freedom."

Tori Jane interrupted, "Next, I'll tell you why we need much stiffer car emission inspections and why SUVs should be banned…"

Ted reached over and turned off the radio.

Officers to Harass

The gate to the resort community swung open.

"Wow, I forgot how nice your place was."

"Yep, I've always loved this escape. And nobody's coming in to see us unless they first get through the gate."

"Don't forget to give the gatekeepers Alice's name."

After winding through thick Pennsylvania woods that hid private rustic getaways, the Goodyears slowly crunched over the stone drive that led to Ben's cedar A-frame.

They unloaded the truck and lit a fire in the fireplace. After strategically placing rifles and shotguns throughout the chalet, they began to unpack and settle in.

Ben was up in the loft, pulling out blankets and towels when there came a knock at the door. Downstairs, Ted drew and held his .45 behind his back; then, cautiously, he opened the door.

There were two men in dark suits holding badges and IDs. The closest one to Ted demanded, "Move your hand from behind your back, sir, and do not produce any weapon. There is a sniper aiming at your head as we speak."

Ted brought his hand forward without his pistol. The agents then padded him down and removed his .45 from under his belt.

Ted bellowed, "Do you really have a sniper out there pointing at my head?"

"No. We just didn't want to get shot. We're only here to talk to you."

Sharply, Ben's voice from the loft demanded, "*Freeze!* There's a loaded twelve-gauge shotgun pointed at *both your heads!*

"Take their weapons and their IDs."

Ted immediately grabbed his own gun back. Reaching under their sport jackets, he removed the agents' two black Sig-Sauer pistols and leather-encased badges.

One of the agents said, "You boys don't know who you're dealing with. We're with the Bureau of—"

Before he could finish, Ben pumped the action of his shotgun and demanded, "Shut up... Pat 'em down for any hideouts."

Ted thoroughly checked them for weapons. Each had a .38 Smith & Wesson Centennial revolver in an ankle holster.

"You boys walk alike, talk alike, look alike, and carry the same guns," chuckled Ted.

Ben directed, "Check their IDs." One read: Agent Carmine Ridge of the Federal Bureau of Investigation. The other: Agent Jonathan Boots from the Bureau of Alcohol Tobacco and Firearms.

"I've never seen agents' IDs. Have you?" Ted asked Ben.

"Call Washington and verify if these guys are really agents or not."

The one named Ridge said, "Look, I'll give you the phone number. You can check—"

"I thought I told you to shut up," reminded Ben. "We don't know who the hell you are, how you got past the gate, or how you even found us here. Just stand there and be thankful that you're not full of buckshot after forcing your way into my community and my house, threatening my friend with a sniper shot to the head and taking his gun!"

Ted called information for the District of Columbia and, after being switched to six different departments, confirmed that Agent Ridge was in fact with the FBI and working special detail with BATF.

"Since apparently you're really FBI and you might be with the Treasury Department," Ben questioned: "What is it that you two want?"

Agent Boots put forth his best officious tone: "We were sent here by the President of the United States of America to propose a special offer to you. We understand that you have in your possession the original Declaration of Independence. The President believes — and so do the polls of Americans questioned about this — that the Declaration belongs to the people and should be returned and properly preserved by the government."

"I don't give a crap about polls or statistics," said Ben. "Statistics are like prisoners of war; they can be made to say anything."

"Well, you're not Mr. Compass, are you?" Agent Boots spoke like a playground bully finally cornered and challenged.

Ted defended, "Ben was my father's friend for over forty years, and has been my friend for my entire life. If there is anyone in this world whom I trust to speak in my name, it's Ben Vernon."

"I'll remember that the next time you tell me to shut up," quipped Ben.

The rotor of a low-flying helicopter shook the chalet.

Ridge and Boots glanced at each other.

Ben and Ted glanced at each other.

Once the reverberations faded, Ted spoke, "Look, I haven't decided what I want to do with the document. I haven't decided *not* to let the government have it. I just would like a little time to think about it. I've been contacted by foreign governments, by foreign auction houses, and by sleazy politicians."

The agents glanced suspiciously at each other again.

"I know one thing for sure," Ted announced: "I don't want any of them to have it. Why don't you arrange for me to meet with the President? I'm willing to work something out. I just don't know what."

"Is it a matter of money? The President has stated that he's willing to meet or top any offer."

"It's not a matter of green or gold. It's a matter of doing the right thing. When may I meet with the President?"

"Give me the phone," said Boots. "I can make arrangements now."

"Make the appointment for three days from today," decided Ted. "I promise I won't do a thing with the document until I first speak with the President."

Ted slipped his .45 back into his holster, walked over and trustworthingly returned the badges and guns to the agents. He handed Agent Boots the telephone — "Make the arrangements."

"Mr. President, the target is still in possession of the item and would like to meet with you in three days to discuss its disposition.... Yes, sir.... Yes, sir... Mr. Compass, the President would like to speak to you directly." Boots handed Ted the phone.

Ted couldn't help but feel a rush: *Wow*, he thought, *the President of the United States needs to talk with me!*

Ted took the phone.

"Hello, am I speaking with Mr. Theodore Compass?"

"Yes."

"I'd like you to know that on behalf of the United States of America, I appreciate your willingness to do your patriotic duty by meeting with me to discuss the appropriate handling of this matter."

"Mr. President, may I ask you one favor?"

"Absolutely, what may I do for you?"

"Would you please guarantee my safety until this matter has been resolved?"

"Surely. Would you like me to assign the agents there to protect you?"

Ted stared at the two agents Ben had just single-handedly disarmed. "No… I would like you to guarantee our safety, but what I would prefer is that absolutely *no* agents or law enforcement come near me or be seen. I am seriously afraid of a double-cross by foreign governments — considering how they have been relentless in trying to contact me. Therefore, with such a guarantee of no agent interference, I would know that anyone who tried to allege that they are from the government would be lying and I could take appropriate action."

"Well, that's an unusual request, but I will order right now that no federal agents, law enforcement, or any parties approach you or where you are in any way. Will you be remaining where you're calling from?"

"Yes, until we come to see you."

"Fine. Please put one of the agents back on the line and I'll begin the arrangements." Ted returned the phone to Agent Boots.

"….Yes, sir, Mr. President, I'll see to it that no one will approach or come near Mr. Vernon or Mr. Compass...." Boots turned to Ted. "The President wants to confirm that you still have the item in your possession."

"I do not have it here or in my possession, but I know where it is. It is still mine and it is still safe."

After hanging up the phone and leaving their business cards on the table, the two agents left the house.

Until the door was shut and locked, Ben never lowered his shotgun.

Safety

"Welcome to *Town Crier*, the nation's most watched and listened to evening-news talk show, broadcast simultaneously by our numerous affiliates in both radio and television around the world and hosted by the award-winning Maxwell Crier."

"Good evening, America, Max Crier here with another edition of *Town Crier*. We have an exclusive tonight. Live via telephone, from a secret location, Mr. Theodore Compass, the man who, yesterday, discovered the original Declaration of Independence when his antique gun exploded. We'll get the whole story, including his recent conversation with the President of the United States, regarding this most important and historic event."

Crier continued: "Open offers have been made for the Declaration: by a prominent rock star who wants to use the Declaration on a concert tour; by the owner of a giant computer company who wants to use the Declaration as the focal point of a new communications museum; and by a Kuwaiti prince who wants to buy the Declaration to gift it back to the U.S. There's also a troubling report that a third-world dictator has offered to buy the Declaration so that he may publicly burn it and another report that a right-wing hate group wants to acquire it as leverage to free their jailed members. It's also been the subject of numerous late night talk-show host monologues. Here's a clip from our very own Ray Beano:

> So, I guess you heard that some guy blew up his rifle and found the original Declaration of Independence. This guy is really amazing, cause that's not all. He blew his nose and out came the missing eighteen-minute gap from the Watergate tapes, Amelia Earhart's plane, and the Vice-President's personality.

Okay — we're not going to break for messages — we're going right to Mr. Compass... Mr. Compass, can you hear me?"

An illustration of a handgun with a Declaration flag coming out of the muzzle (like a "BANG" pistol in a Bugs Bunny cartoon) flashed on-screen whenever Ted spoke. At the bottom of the screen was the statement: "LIVE: THEODORE COMPASS, DISCOVERER OF THE ORIGINAL DECLARATION OF INDEPENDENCE, CALLING FROM AN UNDISCLOSED LOCATION."

"Yes, Max, I'm here."

"Mr. Compass, according to a wire news story first published by the *County News* of New Jersey, you have in fact found the original Declaration of Independence. Is this true?"

"Yes, Max, this is true, and it's been verified."

"I believe Professor Button is on the line now. Dr. Button is a university professor of American history, a noted 'Archeologist of

Americana' who has allegedly examined the document... Professor Button, did you have the occasion to actually examine this document?"

"Yes, I did. And there is no question in my mind as to its authenticity. Furthermore, the Revolutionary War flintlock rifle which contained the Declaration had the initials of the printer, John Dunlap, who was the last known person to possess it."

"That is quite amazing, but I thought the Declaration of Independence was on display and stored in Washington?"

"No," Button replied. "That is actually a printed copy that was signed by the Founding Fathers at later dates. Impressive, but not the one officially approved by Congress in July of 1776."

"Professor, what is this document worth?"

"It's priceless. This was the Holy Grail of American artifacts. How much would you pay for the Holy Grail?"

"Extraordinary! Mr. Compass, are you still on the line?"

"Yes."

"Mr. Compass, how exactly did you find it?"

"Well, I was shooting my antique flintlock at the range when I must have overcharged the gun with too much powder. When I fired it, it blew up and the gun fell from my hands and broke in two. Inside the stock of the rifle was the Declaration."

"Where is it now?"

“I don’t have it with me, but it is in a very safe place which I can access.”

“What are you going to do with it? There’s been a lot of talk that this really belongs to the American people.”

“Max, as an American, I feel the same way. However I want to make sure that it will be properly and safely cared for. My life has been turned upside down since I found it. I will be meeting with the President—”

“Yes, tell us about your conversation with the President of the United States of America.”

“First, let me tell you that I have been contacted by many individuals in regard to the document, including agents of foreign governments, slimeball politicians, and major auction houses. I am afraid that my life is in danger. The President has assured me that he will personally be responsible for my safety and that when I meet with him, I can assure everyone who is listening and watching your show that I will do the proper and morally correct thing.”

“Mr. Compass could you tell us: What is the proper and morally correct thing, in your opinion?”

“Max, I have to go now. But soon all of America will know.”

“No, no, don’t hang up... Did we lose, did we lose Mr. Compass?... Apparently Mr. Compass could no longer stay on the line. But that was an exclusive interview with Mr. Theodore Compass, the discoverer of the original Declaration of Independence which has been lost for over two hundred years. We still have lots of experts, including more discussion with Professor Button and United States Senators Dove and Shears…"

Just then, the television was turned off and Ben walked into the kitchen. "Ted, that was really clever. You now put the President on public notice to protect us. And, yet, we won't be bothered for the next few days. I'll sleep a little bit better tonight."

"I've done my bit for talk shows."

"By the way, what is the 'morally correct' action, Ted?"

"Let's wait for Alice to help figure that one out."

Connections

The evening after Professor Button told him what he possessed, Ted went out and bought oversized see-through document protectors. Now, he finally had time to examine and to better preserve his find.

He snipped off the upper-left corners of the pouches to keep intact the red ribbon that held the pages as one.

He examined each stiff page before sliding it into its protector. Jefferson's handwriting was impressive — perfect, squat cursive text lined each page. *Nobody writes this eloquently anymore, except on wedding invitations.* Ted pondered some of the key words Jefferson had emphasized with capitalizations, such as Infidel, MEN, Liberties, Tyranny, FREE and INDEPENDENT. Before him read the first official usage of the term "United States of America." On the last page, Hancock's signature boldly stretched over four inches long, larger than the famous one and still as artistically blatant.

Firing an original Revolutionary War flintlock was a thrill, but holding and reading the very document touched and discussed over by both Jefferson and Hancock empowered Ted more than any rifle could. This was a metaphysical link through history.

The Spirit of 1776 reached out to Ted. An emotional, protective bond stirred in him similar to when parents first hold their newborn babies. He did not want to part with this document. A multitude of conflicting thoughts, qualms and questions rivered through his mind:

This is too valuable for one man to own

What do I need a billion dollars for?

I must do the morally correct thing.

What is the morally correct thing?

In what direction should I take this?

What do I want?

I want to keep it.

Why can't I keep it?

I should keep it!

What would Jefferson, Adams, Washington or Franklin do?

What would Dad have done?

Intuitively Ted knew he could find one answer that encompassed all of his questions. But he did not yet know how to extract it.

He had glimpsed such an answer in the storm clouds and in the dry grass while on the highway with Ben. He observed the solution in the fervor of gun shows but could not name it. Similarly, he experienced the emotion whenever he protectively slid his .45 into its holster. He treasured such a feeling when he and his father had gone fishing in Alaska's Northwest Passage among the soaring eagles and the surfacing whales.

What was the answer that enveloped all of his questions?

In what direction should I take this?

What is the morally correct thing to do?

He touchstoned the truth the first time he ever voted. He sensed the right thing to do whenever he thought of his grandfather fighting in World War II. He perceived the problem in Ben's anger at illogical radio talk. The solution was apparent when he first got his driver's license and borrowed the family car, when he listened to inspiring music, or when he found himself believing in a well-written story.

Like one of those doors with a short security chain on a slider which first must be closed before opened, the answer had repeatedly revealed itself to Ted yet shut before full disclosure.

What is the answer?

What do I want?...

It was time to unlock and freely open the door.

Happiness

An hour later, a call came from the gate: "Mr. Vernon, a Ms. Alice Rosen is here. However, two federal government agents told us that we're to notify you about anyone coming to your house, and to get your permission or confirmation before letting anyone through. I know you put Ms. Rosen's name down. Do you still want her to visit you?"

"Absolutely, let her in."

"By the way, Mr. Vernon, you can count on us to keep your secret. The agents told us that if we leak this, they would federally prosecute us under Executive Powers. We've put on extra manpower to make sure your privacy is maintained."

"Thank you," stressed Ben. "I'm sorry to impose this on you guys. I should be out of here within the next couple of days."

"As a veteran, this isn't the first time I've put my life on the line defending this. It's not a problem."

Ben opened the front door of the chalet as he watched Alice park her Cadillac beside his Blazer. Striding up to the door, she gave Ben a big kiss on his cheek and lighted, "So, how are the fugitives? While driving in, I heard Ted's interview on the radio."

Alice spoke perfect English with a slight Russian accent. She had come to the U.S. before the collapse of communism in the Soviet Union.

Ted walked out of the bathroom in a clean shirt and voiced, "We're armed and dangerous... Honey, you would not believe the last few days." Resting his hands on her shoulders, Ted stared deeply into Alice's dark, thoughtful eyes and continued, "Boy, am I glad to see you." As the two joyously hugged and kissed, Ben closed and locked the front door.

A sharp French haircut accented Alice's jawline. She hooked the sable locks behind her ears and sighed, "I've been thinking and worrying about you, too, all day. It's a good thing you called me and warned me about what happened. Everyone keeps asking: 'Is that the same Ted Compass I go out with?' People I didn't even know, came up to me and wanted to know all sorts of things about you."

"Hope you didn't tell them anything."

"Only about that cute little mole on your—"

Ted put his hand over her mouth, "Don't go embarrassing Ben, now."

Alice pulled down his hand but still held it, and said, "Let's sit down and talk. Tell me the whole story."

Patient Sufferance

"Sounds like something out of a movie," Alice remarked.

"I know, my head's still spinning."

Ben added, "This has been one hell of a roller coaster ride, and it's not over yet. Teddyboy still has to figure out what he's gonna do with his find."

"Yeah, I know. And I really want to talk to you about that, Al. You have always been able to help me decide things. I have got some ideas; however, this may be the biggest decision I will ever make."

"We have lots of time. Why don't we play some cards and just try to relax."

Ben said, "I don't have any deck of cards. But, there's an old Monopoly game in the closet."

"Monopoly?" bounced Alice. "I love that game, but it always takes too long to play. Finally, enough time to play it right!"

A Monopoly board spread centered on a table by the fireplace. Around it, the trio leisurely rolled dice and sold properties.

Midgame, Ben pondered, "You know, Ted, you could ask for all of *the real* Atlantic City for the Declaration. Or, at least, for one casino... You could buy a whole town. Or, you could start up your own. —*Declaration City?*"

"Yes, I suppose I could. —*Compass*ville? —*Compass* Grove?"

"*Ted*town," threw in Alice.

"I think just plain *Compass*, New Jersey, would be nice," considered Ted, who then joked, "I'd like to have my own exit on the Parkway."

"That would sure make it easy to give directions to your house," stressed Ben. "But, really, what are you going to ask for? A TV station? Stocks and bonds? Tanks, missiles? Airforce One? Or how about lots and lots and lots of tax-free cash?"

"I'm not sure yet."

"You could donate it to the Smithsonian," suggested Alice.

All three quietly looked to each other and, in unison, went "Nahhhhh," shook their heads, and laughed.

"I think you could get a billion dollars," said Ben. "I mean, what's a billion dollars to the U.S. Government? They piss that much away on interest payments for wasteful spending."

"If I asked for anything like that, I would be embarrassed to show my face in the country."

"Yeah, I know what you mean." Ben thought for a moment. "But you'd be embarrassed *in your own* mansion *in your own* town going to *your own* bank."

Ted simply rolled and moved his tophat three spaces. After shuffling through his property cards, he decided, "I'll take another hotel on Park Place." He cashiered out the pastel money to Alice, who was playing banker, and set another hotel onto the crowded board.

Next, Ben rolled, enough to collect two hundred dollars, but ended up going directly to jail.

"Ted, could you loan me a few bucks?"

"I will after I replenish my cash from buying that hotel, okay?"

Unceremoniously, Alice dropped the die to the board and tocked her way across two heavily housed spaces to the safe spot of Community Chest. She reached and removed the top card and stared.

Several silent seconds passed.

The fire reflected in Alice's eyes.

"Alice? What's the matter, Alice?"

Alice held the card in front of her at an angle covering most of her mouth. She shifted her glance from face to face. In a steady low voice she said, "Ted, I know what you should ask for in exchange for the Declaration of Independence."

Ben and Ted chorused: "What?"

She then handed the yellow card to Ted, who silently read it. Ben got out of his chair to read the message over Ted's shoulder.

"What," said Ted, "I don't get it?"

Ben said, "I think I do."

Ted lowered the card face up onto the table. It read:

"GET OUT OF JAIL, FREE."

Pursuing Invariably the Same Object

The Oval Office looked smaller than Ben, Alice and Ted had imagined it. At the edge of the blue carpet, the President greeted them with a smile and an extended hand leading them across the Presidential seal.

"Have a seat. Thank you for coming. I'd like you to meet the Vice-President." The Vice-President rose from a chair beside the President's desk.

There was a brief shaking of hands.

The President moved around his desk and relaxed into his chair. Three seats faced the President.

Ted awed over the chain of events that had led him to be across the desk from the President of the United States of America.

The President leaned forward. "I'm sure you're aware of the media circus surrounding your find. Your discovery has clearly captured the nation's imagination. I purposely have not asked anyone else on my staff to be here so that we could privately discuss how to resolve this matter... Mr. Compass, the original Declaration of Independence is in your possession. The decision as to how we proceed is up to you. On behalf of the United States of America, I officially request that the document be rendered back to the people. What is your position on the matter?"

"Mr. President, Mr. Vice-President, as you both are quite aware, I could sell the original Declaration of Independence for a tremendous sum of money, but that's not what I want. Nor do I want to deprive the American people of their history."

"Glad to hear that, Mr. Compass," happily interjected the President.

"In the time that I've possessed this document, I've had the opportunity to study and to think about its meaning and what I want... What I would request in exchange for the original Declaration of Independence is—

"Freedom."

Both the President and the Vice-President looked at each other, puzzled over the request.

"Freedom?" questioned the President. "You're a citizen of the United States of America, the freest country in the world! 'The Land of the Free.'"

And the Home of the Slave, thought Ben.

"Well, that may be true," replied Ted; "but she's not as free as she once was."

"What do you propose?"

"Let my good friend — and lawyer — Alice Rosen, explain."

Alice coolly pushed herself taller in her chair and informed, "What Mr. Compass seeks is an irrevocable blanket pardon from the United

States of America and all fifty states granting each of the three of us here total immunity from any past or future malum prohibitum offenses or government takings and/or forfeitures in any criminal, quasi-criminal or civil causes of action. This should take the form of a contractual Executive Order."

Alice's clipped accent sparked the fire of her proposal. "If I may, Mr. President, let me clarify. There are two general categories of societal limits on individuals. The two types of laws are best defined for purposes of our discussion as *malum prohibitum* and *malum in se*.

"*Malum in se offenses* are offenses wrong within themselves, such as murder, rape, robbery, morally corrupt crimes, what one would normally think of as common-law crimes. For instance, one doesn't need a legislator to inform us that murder is a crime. That's a malum in se offense.

"*Malum prohibitums*, on the other hand, are offenses created by the legislature, yet there is nothing inherently or intrinsically wrong with them, such as driving safely over a speed limit. Now, of course, if one was to be dangerously out of control at 100 miles per hour or to heedlessly run a red light during rush hour traffic, that would be malum in se and unlawful. Malum prohibitum offenses are mainly consensual or victimless acts that the government has turned into offenses.

"The three of us each want an irrevocable blanket pardon, which would be valid for the rest of our lives and may be passed down to our heirs, which would pardon any past or future *malum prohibitum* offenses and curtail any government takings or forfeiture actions against us. This includes paying all taxes. We want it to cover our organizations, our associates, and/or our agents so that we may conduct business and our personal lives with this same freedom."

Ted interrupted, "The lawyers can work out the details, but essentially you get — without spending a dime — the original Declaration of Independence, and we get what it stands for."

"You wouldn't have to pay taxes and would be immune from federal and state regulations," the President summarized. "But I can probably explain a no-cash deal to the American people a lot easier than I can explain spending a billion dollars." He looked to the Vice-President and asked, "Is there any precedent for a pardon such as this?"

"I don't know, Mr. President. It sounds similar to diplomatic immunity."

Ben reminded, "President Ford gave President Nixon a blanket pardon."

Alice informed, "The power of pardons flows back to the days of monarchies. The sovereign king always has the power to do these types of things. But this isn't just a pardon, it is also a contract between the United States of America and us."

The President paused, then concluded, "I'm sure the details can be hammered out by the lawyers. The good news is, I'll bring the

Declaration of Independence back to the American people. And, I don't need congressional approval for this. I can do this purely by Executive Order. It may take some legislative tweaking and arm-twisting on my part to get the governors to go along, but I'm sure it can be arranged." The President tapped a packet of papers the size of a phone book in front of him on his desk. "See this highway-funding transportation bill? I can pressure any state in the country... I want a formal ceremony in the Rose Garden with the media and top Washington leaders when you hand the original Declaration of Independence to me and I present it back to the American People."

"The ultimate photo-op," the Vice-President quipped.

"Okay then, have your aides contact Ms. Rosen," said Ted, rising from his chair. "She'll handle this for all of us. The next time we meet should be in your Rose Garden after the paperwork has been completed and the pardons are secured."

Alice passed her business card to the President.

Publish and Declare

Pres Brings Declaration Home; Gives Finder, Friends Pardons

WASHINGTON, D.C. – Following weeks of deliberation, the original Declaration of Independence was returned to the People of the United States at a Rose Garden ceremony today.

In exchange, yesterday, the President 'hancocked' wallet-sized pardons to three New Jersey citizens: Alice Rosen, Benjamin L. Vernon, and Theodore E. Compass, who discovered the document when his antique rifle blew up.

To the strains of "The Star Spangled Banner," Compass strode up to the President with a special clear frame containing the Declaration of Independence. The President received the document, shook Compass' hand, and said, "The American people thank you. May the Declaration of Independence and what it stands for live forever in our hearts and minds."

The First Lady said: "My husband – the President who brought the Declaration of Independence home to Washington!"

Compass said that he was pleased with the resolution of the whole matter and that he was proud to be an American.

Pundits have commented that this was one of the greatest public-relations achievements yet for a modern President. Polls show his approval ratings the highest in over two years.

There has been some criticism of the President, however, mostly from Capitol Hill. Democratic Senator Donald Shears, Chairman of the Ethics Committee, today reiterated, "The President only made this deal for political gain. Nothing should have been paid by the United States for something which is rightfully ours to begin with."

Democratic Senator Earl Dove, who also sits on the Ethics Committee, agreed that this matter merits further review.

Nonetheless, the Library of Congress released a short press release ending: "[This] is like a thought-for-dead family member coming home. We are quite indebted to Mr. Compass for rescuing the document."

The pardons Compass and his two friends received give immunity to taxes, government regulation and forfeiture, and past and future "malum prohibitum" offenses (acts that have been prohibited by the legislature). The three are *not* immune for prosecutions of common law crimes such as murder, rape, robbery or assault.

It remains to be seen why Compass chose such a non-monetary reward for the priceless document. Prior to the exchange, Compass' highest offer for the Declaration was rumored to be close to a billion dollars.

Regarding the pardons, Shears said, "I do not believe that such pardons are appropriate or, for that matter, even legal. Congress was never consulted about this. It is wrong to pre-empt the will of the Congress by letting these three ignore laws that the rest of us are forced to obey."

In addition to the President and First Lady, the Vice-President and his wife, Presidential staff and aides, governors, justices, and congressional leaders were all in attendance at today's ceremony.

An equally impressive assemblage is expected next week when Compass will donate his broken flintlock rifle and pieces of the glass tube that held the original Declaration to the museum at Independence Hall in Philadelphia.

Justice and Magnanimity

The place still smells the same, Ben thought as he slid into a counter seat — *burnt bacon, grilled butter, and spilled coffee.* "I'll have the usual," he ordered. "Ham'n cheese, rye toast, hash. And a cup of your freshest, too. Thanks, Bets."

The waitress returned with a carafe of coffee and dropped a handful of creamers. "Haven't been around for a few weeks. Thought maybe we weren't good enough for you anymore since you've become a ce-LEB-rity," Betsy winked.

Ben smiled, "You know I couldn't last long without your coffee and sarcasm."

As she poured, Ben looked up at the scarf wrapped where Betsy's hair should have been. "I'm surprised — but glad — that you're still working here."

"Well, I'm not gonna dwell on my fight. Jim has shortened my hours, but I'm not gonna let The Big C beat me. Except, at times, the chemo really makes me ill."

"I've heard marijuana can help with the pain and sickness. Have you tried?"

"You're not the first to mention that, even today. See that man in the Red Sox cap in the corner booth? He told me he knew where I could get some, but I'm just too afraid."

"Yeah, I understand..." intoned Ben as he picked up his spoon and stirred. Then, conducting the spoon for emphasis, he decided, "Betsy, you've taken good care of me for many years. Let me see if I can serve you this time."

Ben walked his cup of coffee over to the man sitting in the corner booth and sat down in front of him. "Hi, my name is Ben Vernon. I've never seen you in here before."

"Well, I'm from out-of-town."

"Betsy tells me that you know where someone could purchase some special stuff to help her deal with her therapy?" Keeping his eyes forward, Ben sipped from his coffee

"Uh, what are you? A friend of hers?"

"Yes, I've known her for many years, and I'm willing to help her out here."

"You a cop?"

"No, just an old friend of Betsy's."

The man searched Ben's eyes for honesty. After a few seconds, the man reached into his shirt pocket and handed Ben a white card with a phone number on it and nothing else. "Call this number and tell them you're interested in picking up a QP, that's a quarter pound and the only way they sell it, no dime bags or blunts."

Ben didn't know exactly what the man was talking about, but hoped a quarter pound would last Betsy through her therapy.

*

Ben was a little nervous dealing with people he didn't know in a low-rent motel room. He hadn't actually tested out his pardon yet, either; however, he knew that with his new-found freedoms the purchase was legal. When the man with the buzz-cut and gold earring concluded, "That'll be four hundred bucks," it seemed as though the deal would go through without a hitch.

After pocketing Ben's cash in exchange for a bag of chopped green leaf, the seller pointed at Ben's rifle club shirt. "Hey, you like guns?"

"Yep."

"Let me show you a really neat piece."

Ben tugged at the visor of his baseball cap, "Sure, okay."

From under the bed the man slipped out a case, unzipped it, and extracted an M3 Greasegun in .45 caliber. He offered the sub-machine gun over for Ben to hold.

"Oh man, I carried one of these in Korea!" Ben checked the action. "I loved that gun. It was crude but effective. I always wanted to have one of my own, too."

"Well, here's your chance. Five hundred. No fuss, no muss. No questions asked."

Ben strode out of the motel with a cased M3 Greasegun in one hand and a brown paper bag containing a QP of marijuana in the other. He tucked the brown bag under the arm holding the case, took out his keys, and opened his passenger side door. After dropping both items onto the seat, he walked to the driver's side and started his truck. As he was about to drive away, three police cars with blaring lights barricaded him. Two cops ran to each door with pistols drawn. One shouted, "You are under arrest for unlawful purchase and possession of a CDS and a sub-machine gun! Step out of your vehicle."

Another snickered, "Now we can seize and forfeit your truck, too, 'cause we waited till you got in it!"

"What's a CDS?" Ben calmly asked as he shifted his car back into park.

"Controlled Dangerous Substance— and we'll ask the questions, not you. Step out of the car." Ben's hat was knocked off his head as he was pulled out of his seat (apparently he wasn't moving fast enough). Ben was told to put both hands onto the hood and forced to spread his legs for a pat-down search.

Ben matter-of-factly stated, "You boys are making a big mistake."

Suddenly, the cop patting him down yelled, "Hey, this guy's carrying a gun! — I mean, *another* gun," and removed Ben's trusty .45 from his belt. "You're in even more trouble now."

"No, you're in big trouble now," flatlined Ben.

"Yeah, what's that supposed to mean? You threatening me?" barked the officer apparently in charge of the operation.

"He's pretty calm for a man facing twenty-five years in jail," said the younger officer who had patted him down and was now searching his glove compartment.

The officer-in-charge proceeded, "You have the right to remain silent. Anything you say can and will be used against you. You have the right to an attorney. If you cannot afford one, one will be appointed for you. Do you understand these rights?"

"Yeah. My name is Benjamin Vernon. I understand my rights but I don't think you do — I have immunity granted to me by the President of the United States of America and by the governor of this state allowing me to acquire anything I want. You boys are now on notice as to who I am and I would respectfully suggest that you release me at once. Check inside my wallet which you just put on top of the car."

An officer opened the wallet and said, "Hey, I remember hearing about this guy. He cut that special deal and has this special immunity card. Better call headquarters to check it out..."

With a foot on the fender of his Blazer, Ben casually leaned on his knee. He was chatting with the four officers left to guard him about cutting his deal with the President and about all of the Washington big shots he met at the Rose Garden Ceremony. When the officer-in-charge walked back from his patrol car, he humbled, "We're terribly sorry, Mr. Vernon. We didn't realize who you were. Here's your nine hundred dollars back."

"No thanks," said Ben. "I want what I lawfully purchased."

"What do ya mean?"

"My marijuana, my Greasegun and, of course, my custom .45 you removed from my belt, please."

"What!?"

"Look, I lawfully purchased the pot and the Greasegun and I don't accept a refund for your attempted robbery. If you push this issue, not only will I sue you for harassment, false arrest, false imprisonment and illegal search, but for breech of contract as well. And, you can explain to the President of the United States of America why you ignored his Executive Order."

The head officer scratched just under the brim of his cap and glanced to the other officers, all of whom had no answers. He reluctantly treaded to an undercover van at the far corner of the parking lot and back again with a full duffel bag.

The man sighed, "I can't believe I'm doing this." From the canvas, he handed Ben the bag of marijuana and the Greasegun, which Ben returned to his passenger seat.

Next, the officers handed Ben his .45 in one hand and the loaded magazine in the other. Ben thrust the magazine into the magwell with a confident click. The policemen watched powerlessly as Ben racked the slide and raised the safety, placing his .45 in condition one, cocked and locked.

While getting into his Blazer, Ben reholstered his loaded pistol and remarked, “Thank you, officers.” As he shut the door, he added, “Have a nice day.”

The happy customer waved and grinned as he drove off to give Betsy her medicine.

The head officer shook his head, wondering how he was going to explain to the brass the department’s sale of pot and a Greasegun.

To Alter or To Abolish

While Ben was enjoying some personal freedoms to help others and himself, Alice was working on a blueprint to change the world. She had a general objective before she ever put forward the deal with the President, however she had not worked out the specific way to implement her concepts.

Alice told the love of her life that she needed a weekend alone to outline her game plan. Ted understood perfectly, having recently escaped to decide his own future.

Alice fixed herself a cup of herbal tea and settled into her favorite Lay-Z-Boy.

She thought to herself: *How would Dagny Taggart handle this?*

Dagny Taggart is the main character of Atlas Shrugged by Ayn Rand. Rand's writings and philosophies had first inspired Alice in communist Russia when, as a teenager, she read a smuggled copy of the lengthy, pro-capitalist book. Alice's father was proud of her; in their Leningrad home, Pappa Rosen required that only English be spoken. He knew that one day his family would immigrate into the United States of America.

In Atlas Shrugged, the greatest thinkers and doers on Earth go on strike and, in effect, stop the motor of the world.

But I don't want to stop the motor of the world... I want to turbo-charge *it!*

When the deal was cut with the President, Alice made sure that she had the power to eliminate the blanket of government oppression from herself and for others.

But how could such a plan be effectively implemented? And where should I start?

Theoretically, why would the greatest minds in the world even consider going on strike?

Because of the curtailment of their freedoms and the disappropriation of their money, property, ideas and labor — That's why!

What is it that prevents American business from being the best that it can be?

American business is in bondage by way of red-tape bureaucracies, burdensome taxes, unreasonable regulations and out-of-control tort laws — That's what!

Alice was determined to diminish — if not to destroy — those impediments to American business and to help Ted, Ben, herself and America in the process.

Before falling asleep in her recliner, Alice pared it down to one issue:

How can three people with the Midas Touch of Freedom put that power to use whereby both they and the world would benefit?

The next morning while in the shower the answer came to her. And it wasn't all that complicated either.

Her plan consisted of a one-two punch:

First: an example.

Then: an invitation.

To Prove This

"Hello, this is Alice Rosen. How've you been, George?"

"I've been fine, but I've heard *you've* been quite busy lately," understated the voice on the other end. "Are you calling to buy?"

"Yes. Well actually, today I'd like to make a slightly unusual stock purchase: three shares of Eureka Medical Technologies."

"Only three shares?" squalled George. "Eureka Med? I don't advise it. That company is having all sorts of trouble with the FDA over radical medical treatments."

"Their ideas make a lot of sense to me."

"Yeah, yeah, I've read about them, too; but they have to get over tons of bureaucratic hurdles — some of their drugs are not even approved yet in Europe — To get really cooking, that'll take years. You'll never see worthwhile profit from just three shares anyway. It'll cost that much just to do the transaction. Although, I understand your sentiments, especially if you've got a sick friend."

"I'd like to make a stock purchase of three shares of Eureka Medical Technologies;" Alice affirmed, then softened, "but thanks for the advice, anyway."

"Okay, three shares, Eureka."

"Only one share is for me, though."

"You've got to be kidding!"

"No. The other two shares I'd like to be put separately under the names of two friends…"

Pressing Importance

BUSINESS REPORT:

Med Stock Soars After 'Private' Deregulation

EDISON, New Jersey – You're shouting *Eureka!* if you're holding their stock.

Eureka Medical Technologies has not only developed potential cures for a number of immune deficiency and hepatitis diseases [see Health & Science, D1] but they've also found the cure to avoid cumbersome government regulations.

Eureka Med was fortunate in that Alice Rosen – one of 'The Freedom Three' to receive controversial governmental pardons awarded in exchange for the original Declaration of Independence last week – bought three shares of their company.

Although critics argue that some people may be injured or even die in the long-term because of Eureka's radical treatments, others argue that their treatments at least offer hope.

Eureka Medical Technologies President, Dr. Samuel Hart said, "Ms. Rosen chose and contacted us – And boy, are we glad she did! We were doing our best to comfort and to cure individuals with deadly diseases, but you know how the system works... She apparently recognized, on her own, what was holding us back from being the best pharmaceutical company we could possibly be. Now, the sky's the limit!"

"Stock represents partial ownership in a company," Rosen explained. "Shares in pardoned individuals' names allow a company to remove itself from excessive government regulations and taxation."

Rosen continued, "If there is any other company in the United States that wishes not to be subjected to governmental regulations and taxations, I invite it to issue at least one share of stock in my name, one in Mr. Theodore Compass' name, and one in Mr. Benjamin Vernon's name. After all three of us have been issued stock, I will send out a Memorandum of Agreement explaining in more detail what the companies may do under their newly-found deregulation and freedom from taxation."

For more information go to www.revtwo.com.

Civil Power

"Poppity, pop, pop, pop! Pop! Pop! Poppity-pop-pop-pop! Pop!!"

Ben fitted the yellow-banded Cohiba that just lit the pack of firecrackers back into the corner of his mouth. After savoring a puff, he explained to the group of neighborhood kids circling around him: "This is how we celebrated the Fourth of July when I was a teenager. Of course, I didn't smoke cigars as a boy." *But, back then, fireworks and Cuban cigars were legal*, he thought.

"May I try lighting a firecracker?"

"How 'bout me?"

"Can I light one?"

"Sure, everyone will light some as long as I'm here supervising," Ben preached. "Remember: Safety first. Never use fireworks without an adult around."

Just then, a few of the kids warned, "Here come the cops, Mr. Vernon! Here come the cops."

A ten-year-old girl piped: "My daddy said firecrackers are illegal in New Jersey. Are they going to arrest you?"

Before Ben could answer, the police car pulled up and the officer lowered her window. She recognized Ben's friendly round face from the police briefing that the entire department had received. She also knew him as a regular at Jimbo's Bite Shop.

"Oh, it's you, Mr. Vernon. Enjoy your Independence Day," she smiled and drove on.

Ben puffed and howled: "Next — Bottle rockets!"

The ever-growing crowd of kids cheered.

Declare the Causes

The television screen showed the outside of the Law Offices of Alice Rosen, Attorney and Counselor at Law. The picture then switched to an inside conference room where a blonde woman and a brunette woman faced each other in leather-backed chairs. "Welcome to *Financial World Special Report* with Dolly Larson," intoned over the image.

In a close-up, the thin-lipped blonde in a business suit prefaced: "As I'm sure you know, America is experiencing a charging bull market lately. Over the past week, a phenomenon has taken hold of American business and the American people—

"And her name is Alice Rosen."

The monitor switched to a headshot of Alice with rows of symmetrical law books behind her, then back to Larson.

"Tonight we feature an on-location interview with the woman who has single-handedly penned new chapters in the books of business and social history, ironically with a sort of 'eraser.' Thanks to a recent Presidential pardon, Ms. Rosen has, company-by-company, enabled corporate America to generate, to produce, and to take actions which have long been stifled. This has occurred through what pundits call 'private deregulation.'

"Ms. Rosen has been able to hoist up the white flag on the war on drugs. She has created a legalized sexual services market for adults who are free of sexually transmitted diseases. And, with black market profits virtually eliminated and law-abiding citizens across the country legally carrying concealed firearms and other weapons, the violent crime rate has dropped to an all-time low.

"Rent decontrol and tax elimination are just two of the controversial economic changes taking place in America. Apartment construction starts are growing so fast that rents are predicted to drop for the first time since rent-control was first established over fifty years ago...

"Ms. Rosen, what do you hope to accomplish through your recent nonconformist actions?"

"My goal is to stop Americans from becoming victims of victimless crimes and to spark the Second Industrial Revolution."

Ms. Larson tilted her head and widened her eyes like an inquisitive puppy. "What do you mean by this?"

"America will become an industrial economic powerhouse the likes of which the world has never seen, the potential of which was always there."

Larson tilted her head to the opposite side. "America already is the leading super power."

"Let's not become complacent and overly confident. The United States is threatened, economically challenged, by other world powers, such as China, Japan, Indochina, the developing Europe, and even by emerging third-world economies such as Mexico." Alice's Russian inflections only strengthened the preceding statement. "The reason for America's original success was business freedom — and it is a formula which works."

"The Industrial Revolution at the Turn of the Century included robber-barons," argued Larson. "Aren't they inherent in such a Revolution?"

"The so-called 'robber' barons such as Carnegie and Rockefeller all realized the benefits of philanthropy both to others and to themselves. The quality of life that we currently enjoy can be directly accredited to their talents and efforts as the most successful businessmen the world has ever known. I'll take robber barons over Big Brother any day. As leaders of American industry, barons provide the means for our workforce to create and produce. Without our first Industrial Revolution and the freedoms that allowed it to occur, we would be a third-world nation."

"But, our natural resources—"

"The wealth of a nation," Alice cut short, "is not solely determined by its gold or by other natural resources but rather by its capital and by its tools of production. —Economics 101, Adam Smith, *Wealth of*

Nations. What natural resources does Japan have? Yet, Japan is clearly an industrial nation with a high standard of living. On the other hand, African states are rich in natural resources, including people, but not in the tools of production; overall, their standard of living is low compared with industrialized nations. With my help, America's tools of production will metaphorically change from handsaws to powersaws, from hammers to nailguns. I want to see the United States progress to the *next* higher level and set a *new, unequaled* standard for quality of life."

Alice sat firmly in her seat, only occasionally leaning forward and offering simple open-palmed gestures for emphasis.

Larson spread out her hands to discourage Alice from cutting her off again and continued, "Ms. Rosen, child labor laws were also a result of the Industrial Revolution."

"Are you inferring that with all the inner-city violence, today's youth would not be better off working and making money? Instead of admiring the local petty hoodlum or drug dealer, out-of-school teenagers are now wanting to become part of America's workforce and achieve honest financial success."

"But who's going to protect the children?" Larson demanded.

"How about: their parents? Furthermore, workers are free to unionize and criminals will no longer be kids' role models. My plan eliminates the war on drugs."

"Several tobacco companies have announced plans to market marijuana. Doesn't this mean children will have easier access to drugs," countered Larson.

"How is marijuana — or any drug for that matter — any worse than alcohol? You can overdose on alcohol, suffer psychiatric consequences from alcohol, become addicted to alcohol… And, alcohol is far deadlier than marijuana. The law is even stopping hemp, one of the world's best natural fibers, from being grown. The key isn't a substance, but irresponsible usage. I'm working on taking the profit out of illegal drug trafficking. With just the announcement alone, street prices of drugs have dropped. Organized crime, drug dealers, drug gangs, the PBA, criminal defense attorneys, and corrupt politicians are very upset about the legalization of drugs. Drug dealers are the hardest hit by the decriminalization of recreational drugs. They are being forced to find real jobs now. If an inner-city youth wants to become wealthy, he or she will now see the obvious path is through brainpower, education, work, industry and individual achievement."

"Unless they're shot first!" Larson sarcastically interjected. "Haven't your efforts put more guns on the streets?"

"Yes, but in the right hands. Citizens may now protect themselves as intended by the Second Amendment, whereas before it was only the criminals, who ignored the gun control laws, who were armed."

"So you would have no objection to someone owning, say, a nuclear weapon if they wanted to?"

"I would most certainly object. A nuclear weapon is a weapon of *mass* destruction, not personal defensive armament. Historically, canons and other offensive weapons of mass destruction were owned by *the community*. The right to keep and bear arms was intended to guarantee people having the right to personal defensive weapons that they can individually possess and carry. Our founding fathers, Jefferson, Washington, Henry, Mason, all defended themselves, their families and our country with firearms. And it's even more important today since they had more closely knit communities in the 1700s."

"Well, Ms. Rosen, let's get back to your economic policies... The Industrial Revolution also brought with it monopolies and trusts and cartels, all of which tried to fix prices."

"Like breaking up the phone company really worked?" Alice sarcasmed. "I'm not saying we're going to live in a utopia — in fact, I wouldn't want to live in most of the 'utopias' I've read about — but, at least, we will not have abandoned and turned into a lie our fundamental belief in freedom and equality. We will no longer be living under some bastardized form of socialism. Any system we choose has down sides. If our system must err, let it err on the side of freedom."

"No Affirmative Action? No minimum wage?"

"Racial, sexual and other discriminations are luxuries businesses cannot afford. Already there is a tremendous demand for employment. And negative unemployment, of course, means higher salaries. We may yet have fair competition with other countries. We may actually be building some American cars in America again. Our economic strength and growth will help America overcome all of its current social problems."

"How do you propose we pay for our government without taxes?"

"The government may charge for some of the services it renders. For example, if two parties want a contract to be enforceable, they should have to pay a judicial fee to register their contract. Why should the government enforce business contracts for free? As income taxes and regulations have been eliminated for those corporations to which I am associated, government's role has conversely been severely reduced. Obviously, we don't need an overburdening bureaucracy or to pay for one."

"In fact," Larson informed, "government regulators are in a state of panic over their usurped powers."

"Jobs await those individuals in private industry."

"Industries such as prostitution?" Larson controversially interjected.

"You mean what's commonly referred to as 'the oldest profession?' Just because America is sexually repressed doesn't mean we have to criminalize sex between consenting adults simply because money is involved. It is not surprising that all our anti-prostitution laws have failed as miserably as our anti-drug laws. Companies that I own stock in are now providing sexual services in a professional and health-conscious manner. Prostitution has been legal in some Nevada counties for years and in jurisdictions of Europe and Asia for centuries. It's time we stop persecuting Americans for consensual sex.

"By the way," Alice added. "I am also affiliating myself with as many gun clubs and associations as possible, thereby empowering members to be exempt from firearm regulations. Affiliated gun owners are now able to purchase, carry and possess firearms without the government being involved."

"Any other surprises in store for us?"

"Yes. I would personally like to see income tax eliminated for individuals as it has been for Ted Compass, Ben Vernon, and myself. The United States of America got along fine for one hundred years without an income tax, you know?"

"Government was a lot simpler back then."

"Exactly."

Larson changed her tact: "You talk of America as if you've lived here your whole life, though you haven't. Your family immigrated here from Russia when you were just a teen. Aren't you tearing up the very fabric of America with all these drastic changes?"

"No, I'm *mending* the holes in the fabric made by those who have attacked industry and individual autonomy, the two principles on which America was founded, made expansion and growth possible, and why my father brought his family here in the first place. Our freedoms should not be limited by society's lowest common denominator. Just because the village idiot can't handle a certain liberty, doesn't mean that responsible adults must give up that freedom. This is reminiscent of the old Hicklin Obscenity Laws which argued that since children and the mentally challenged shouldn't view pornography, mature adults must also be restrained. The media and the intellectual elite successfully opposed these speech restrictions; but then they applied the Hicklin principle to rights they do not understand or do not desire themselves... And, by the way, Patrick Henry didn't arrive in America until just *two* years before the American Revolution."

Larson simply posed another question, "How do you propose to pay for the necessities government does provide?"

"Government functions should mostly rely on self-financing. I don't have a problem with the government making a profit either. If an individual needs government services, he or she should have to pay for it or go to private parties. Considering how much more disposable income the American people are going to have during this economic boom, I am confident that American generosity, as it always has, will fund any programs it considers worthwhile. Most citizens already do support non-profit organizations they consider important such as public radio, public television, homeless shelters, volunteer fire and first aid services... We've traditionally given tax exemptions to religious and social welfare charities. Such tax exemptions have proven extremely successful and stand as prototype models bolstering my position."

Alice continued metaphorically, "People and businesses have been kept in jail for so long, many are afraid to leave even when the prison gate is left wide open. They consider the cell to be home because they have been in it so long, like a dog demanding that it be put in its cage each night because it's so used to sleeping there, like an elephant hitched only by a loosely looped rope…"

"Those are definitely some heavy duty comparisons. Are we no better than animals?"

"My point exactly. We are not animals and shouldn't be treated as such."

"Is America ready for this?"

"The question is: Is it too late for this?"

"As you probably already know," informed Larson lifting a magazine article in one hand, "the Senate Ethics Committee, chaired by Senator Donald Shears, has decided to investigate the propriety and impact of the President's immunity actions which, through you, are so radically altering our society." At the top of the article was a dark closeup photo of Senator Shears open-mouthed and flailing his arms over a podium. "What are your thoughts on this?"

"See those crates marked 'Property of U.S. Post Office?'" Alice pointed across the room. The camera panned to ten, full, stacked white crates. "Those are filled with companies which sent stock certificates that I haven't reviewed yet. Obviously, corporations are thrilled and excited about having their freedoms restored."

Alice next pointed to the other side of the room. "See those crates piled there? They're full of letters, telegrams and faxes of appreciation from Americans thanking me for restoring their rights and hopes. I have given people newfound freedoms to make choices without the fears of government persecutions over those choices. Senator Shears is a hypocritical, elitist, authoritarian politician. He is scared of giving back to America freedoms that he helped to eliminate in order to further empower himself. Any critics I may have apparently don't want America to be as economically strong as she could be or her people as free as they could be."

"Why should a business make you and your associates shareholders and get involved with all this controversy?"

"By making my friends and me shareholders, a company gets to share in our immunities. These immunities address fundamental issues facing American business. The question for American business is simple: Are they interested in eliminating the IRS, the EPA, the

Commerce Department, the Department of Health, Education and Welfare, the EEOC, the FDA, BATF, OSHA, the whole host of bureaucratic alphabet soup from their business activities? If the answer is yes, then they will follow in the path of Eureka Medical Technologies."

"And if the answer is no?"

"Then they are doing business in the wrong country."

"It is my understanding that you are a recent shareholder of our broadcasting corporation, Financial World Enterprises."

"Yes, I'm sure that has a lot to do with the three letters: F-C-C."

"Thank you, Ms. Alice Rosen, for being our guest today. Is there anything else you would like to add?"

"Yes, anybody watching this program who is interested in becoming a participant in America's Second Industrial Revolution may access further information at my website."

At the bottom of the screen flashed:

www.revtwo.com.

A Design to Reduce Them

The lights were dim in Senator Shears' conference room. In a black, pinstriped suit, the Senator sat at the head of a long table with a thumb hooked in the front of his belt. Rubbing his other palm along his cigar-ash shock of hair, Shears demanded, "Okay, Boots, Ridge, show me what you got."

Boots pressed the remote control in his left hand. A television set at the opposite end of the table flickered with movement. Boots paused the screen on a closeup of Ben about to puff on a Cohiba cigar. "That's Benjamin L. Vernon. Mid-sixties, six-foot two, 250 pounds. Gray hair, blue eyes. Heterosexual. Born: Monmouth County, New Jersey. Current residence: still Monmouth County. Owns alternate house in the Poconos. Drives: red Blazer. One traffic accident, five years ago. Twelve registered handguns and a state firearm identification card. High school graduate with vocational training. Retired construction worker. Annual income last year: $35,000. Awarded Silver Star in Korea. Honorable Discharge. Widowed, no kids. Liked by neighbors — one of whom stated, 'If I ever have a problem, I can count on Ben to help me out.' — Hospitalized once for broken leg, once for appendectomy, once for stomach virus. Takes medication daily to lower blood pressure. Likes: hunting, fishing, cigars, movie classics. NASCAR racing fan, successful IPSC competitor."

"What's ip-sick?" asked the Senator.

"I-P-S-C is an acronym for the International Practical Shooting Confederation. Competitors draw and fire handguns in realistic scenarios…" Boots resumed the video: "This was filmed in a bar near Vernon's home in New Jersey. As you can see here, Senator, he is approached by a high-priced call girl. If you listen closely through the bar noise, you can hear her saying—" Boots read flatly from his clipboard. "—I know you. You're Ben Vernon. You can pay me to do it with you and it's not illegal, right?' Mr. Vernon replied, 'Yes, that's true.' However, more blatantly — I'll fast forward to it now, sir — later that night, at the same bar, another person came up to him and demonstrated a switchblade knife, which Mr. Vernon bought from him for seventy-five dollars. It was a high quality Benchmade automatic, normally restricted to law enforcement and military personnel. In fact, our information has uncovered that Mr. Vernon has purchased various weapons, including an M3 Greasegun, a flame thrower—"

"Flame thrower?" interrupted Shears.

"Yes," continued the agent. "And a wrist-rocket slingshot, many unregistered handguns and assault firearms, and various explosives, including firecrackers and bottle rockets."

"He's the only guy in Jersey with a rifle rack hanging in his truck," added Ridge. Looking back down to his clipboard: "Through the mail he's ordered hardcore pornographic video tapes, a black powder pistol, and a high-powered Barnett crossbow with poison-capacity bolts."

"What the hell are poison-capacity bolts?" again interrupted Shears.

"Bolts are short arrows. These bolts hold a type of poison primarily used for deer hunting down South," informed Boots.

Flipping through his report, Ridge added: "Then there's several boxes of Cuban cigars. A quarter-pound of marijuana. Three slot machines — which he stores in his garage—"

"He's been pulled over three times for speeding and was not issued a single ticket," Boots piped in. "He drives like a cop and rides his motorcycle without a helmet."

"And he's built a barbecue pit in his back yard without a building permit," Ridge returned. "Basically, Senator, a lot more of the same..."

"But here, however…" Boots fast-forwarded. "Next on the video, you'll see Alice Rosen, who's wrecking havoc with our business interests. Here she is on Dolly Larson's *Financial World*—"

"I know all about *her*," the Senator sneered.

"What you may not fully know, though, sir," noted Ridge, "is that she has an advanced degree in finance and has masterminded an ownership interest in nearly every U.S. corporation. In fact, some companies which were privately held are making Rosen, Vernon and Compass limited partners or issuing exclusive securities just to welcome the three of them into their businesses. Rosen's, Vernon's and Compass' stock portfolios are worth millions of dollars... and growing."

The room was silent.

"Okay, what about my primary concern: Mr. Compass?" Shears demanded.

Boots again methodically responded from his clipboard: "Theodore E. Compass. Early-thirties, six-foot three, 200 pounds. Heterosexual. Dark red hair, brown eyes. Also, born, raised and currently living in New Jersey. Only child. His mother, a cashier, was killed during a 1972 attempted robbery of a convenience store. Father, a construction worker, never remarried and died of natural causes two years ago. Masters degree in Engineering from New Jersey Institute of Technology. President of Compass Engineering, Incorporated, which grew out of his father's construction company. Annual income last year: $75,000. Instrumental in the design and construction of the Chamberlain Bridge and the Goldwater Scenic Highway, among other civil projects. Five registered handguns, at least one shotgun. State firearm ID card. Never been hospitalized. Books taken out of the library within the last two years show concentrations in history, art and science. He has been romantically linked with Alice Rosen since grad school—"

With a fist to the table, Shears cut off the litany. "What I want to know is: What has he been up to since cutting his deal with the President!"

"He's a mystery," remarked Boots. "The man who started all this by discovering the original Declaration of Independence seems to be taking the least advantage of the immunities granted him."

Ridge chimed, "The only thing we have on Compass is that he failed to pay a ticket for not wearing a seat belt, which a judge has subsequently dismissed."

Shears snickered, "Keep an even closer tab on *him*! There must be something really heavy that he's keeping concealed and waiting to expose... We are going to slam the door on these three. They are the primary threat to all our financial interests. Their actions are severely damaging our associates' drug, gambling and prostitution operations. Now, with citizens carrying guns, even our protection rackets are being hurt. My backers and business partners are furious that their once illegal trades are being eliminated. This has been the worst thing for them since the repeal of Prohibition! Vernon, Rosen and Compass haven't left a single profitable U.S. business avenue open.

"A deregulated United States has also struck fear into our foreign interests," Shears hissed. "They report that business competition is now going to be impossible with the regulations lifted. They worked damn hard and invested large sums of money to see these restrictions implemented to cripple American businesses. Foreign contributors to my campaign war chest are bailing out on me."

The reconnaissance video played on showing Ted, wearing shorts and a Disney World T-shirt, watering the lawn in front of his home.

Getting his anger under control, Shears encouraged, "Keep up the good work and you two will still soar like arrows up the ranks. And have no fear, your offshore bank accounts will continue to grow. I will try to use my position and power as a senator to eliminate these three jokers. They don't know who they're screwing with. I want Vernon, Rosen and Compass watched twenty-four/seven."

"Yes, sir," snapped Ridge.

"Our pleasure, boss," added Boots. Ridge finished, "Our intelligence reports that Compass and Vernon will be going fishing tomorrow. We'll be sure to apply full surveillance."

Pursuit of Happiness

"Sorry I'm late, Ted. The president of our gun club called me just as I was about to leave," Ben explained as Ted opened his front door. "Some anti-gun councilmen are trying to close down our target range by passing ridiculous noise ordinances even though our club has been there for fifty years. Since we're vested members, we're able to save the club from being shut down. *Three cheers for us!*"

Ben sported a khaki vest and a wrinkled boonie hat with fishing lures hooked to it. As Ted locked up his house, Ben continued, "Blowing up your rifle was the best mistake you have ever made. And if it wasn't for the club, you wouldn't have had such a great place to do it."

"Being late is no problem," answered Ted as he walked over to his garage door and lifted it. "I was just watching the morning news. Alice was on again. She's really got people stirred up. Today's report featured a parochial school teacher who is finally getting paid on a competitive pay scale, a grocer who could at last put up advertisement signs in his windows, an owner of a health food store whom the FDA no longer intimidates, a reverend who was relieved that the BATF won't turn his parish into another Waco, a police officer whose paperwork has been cut in half and another officer who was glad she could at last go after 'real criminals' — All praising Alice."

"That girl is something else. My portfolio looks amazing. She's provided me with a financial umbrella for the rainiest economic day I could ever imagine. I'm glad *she* can keep it all straight."

"Well, she really wants America to return to its former glory she remembers secretly learning about while in Russia," summarized Ted as he lowered a fishing rod and tackle box from a shelf. "By the way, we're celebrating our restored freedom by finally returning to Williamsburg for a vacation next month." Ted pulled at a plastic envelope attached to his rod-and-gun club jacket and laughed, "Even though I didn't have to, I bought a fishing license. Some of the money pays for conservation."

"Think the Indians got a license before they went fishing?" answered Ben as Ted shut and locked the garage. "I'm never paying for another damn license for anything for the rest of my life. The government can kiss my—"

"Come on, let's hit the lake."

"What? I was gonna say *bass*."

Ben and Ted rowed to a place a few yards offshore where a line of pines threw shadows on the water, where they could work a good bait. The two sat shoulder-to-shoulder on swivel seats facing opposite directions.

Ben held up the end of his line. "See this lure I just tied on?"

Ted leaned back to see. "Yeah?"

"See that end I have to cut?"

"Yeah."

Ben reached inside his jacket and pulled out a pocketknife. With a press of a button, he was able to cut the line without letting go of the lure or of the pole. "Isn't this switchblade great? Can you believe these things used to be illegal for us to own? What was the big deal?"

"How 'bout cutting mine?" Ted nodded, holding taut his line.

"I told you that story about the Greasegun and the pot, right?" asked Ben as he cut.

"Yeah, that was a hoot. Glad the card worked. First try, right?"

Ben took a sip from his beer and said, "Yep, worked like a charm. Have you taken advantage at all of your pardon?"

"Nothing major."

With a flick of his wrist, Ted's fishing line whipped the air above the lake. "You know, Ben. Believe it or not, just knowing that I am free and knowing that I can do what I want, whenever I want, without fear of government interference is the greatest comfort to me. I feel wonderful just knowing I am free. It's a mental thing. I sleep better. My digestion's better. This whole experience has had a physical effect on me. It feels as if a great weight has been lifted off my shoulders."

"It has," Ben confirmed, reeling in his line. "It has."

The aluminum boat rocked with an easy creak. Ted keenly inhaled the calming lake air, then pondered, "You know, I'm not really interested in using drugs. I'm not interested in soliciting a prostitute. I'm not interested in most activities that were once illegal for me. However, I do like pumping my own gas, making rights on red in any state I visit, and not paying use taxes. Just knowing that the Internal Revenue Service can't foreclose on my house, or that the Bureau of Alcohol, Tobacco and Firearms isn't going to turn me into a criminal by declaring some gun I own illegal, or that the Environmental Protection Agency isn't going to make me throw out my gas lawnmower or my barbecue are tremendous reliefs. I don't worry whether my driver's license has expired or if my car needs to be inspected for some arbitrary emissions check. I love the fact that I may ride my bike without a helmet if I want some easy wind in my hair. And I no longer have to pay into that government-run, pyramid scheme: Social Security. I can invest for my retirement however I see fit. I'm not just a number anymore... All that excessive mothering and those stupid, time-consuming bureaucratic annoyances were draining away my rights to 'life, liberty, and pursuit of happiness.'"

"We're living the ideal of the Declaration of Independence," Ben explained. "I wouldn't trade this freedom for a billion dollars, either."

"Yeah, even wealthy and famous people couldn't buy the freedoms that are once again emerging throughout the land. Take, for instance, rich and well-known entertainers like Lenny Bruce or Christian Slater who have been arrested and dragged through the system and through the media for absurd malum prohibitum offenses."

"Yeah, remember how they arrested and maligned Robert Mitchum for marijuana?" reminded Ben.

"They did the same thing to Paul McCartney, and to David Crosby, and to Jerry Garcia. Tim Allen and Don King got busted for drugs before they became famous."

"And that actor who played Charlie Chaplin, Robert Downey, Jr., was arrested for drugs, too."

"I remember when that professional tennis player — What was her name? — got into legal trouble for drug possession."

"And Keith Hernandez. And other Mets, too."

"Darryl Strawberry, for drugs and for soliciting a prostitute. Yankee Joe Pepitone, for gun and drug problems... And a slew of Dallas Cowboy football players."

"Hugh Grant also, for prostitution."

"Jim Morrison and Janis Joplin were prosecuted for obscenity."

"George Carlin, too."

"Jose Conseco got into trouble for speeding."

"Yeah, like David Letterman."

“The list goes on and on,” noted Ted. “They were all screwed for malum prohibitums, for possessing items that we may now lawfully possess or for doing things that we may now lawfully do.”

“And look what the IRS did to Willie Nelson… No money or fame could stop the system from putting them all through the shredder and messing up their lives,” concluded Ben.

“Yeah, I finally know what it means to be free,” sighed Ted. “I know what it means. I feel born again: more positive, more outgoing, more self-confident. I even feel a renewed pride in being an American citizen.”

“Of course, you’re right. Me, too. I’ve just had a little fun pushing the envelope with what I may personally do. And I haven’t hurt anybody either. In fact, I may have even helped a few. Even though I’ve been free two whole months, can you believe I’m not addicted to heroine or cocaine?” Ben joked.

“And I’m not shouting curse words around the town?” added Ted.

“And I’m not parading nude down the highway.”

“Or driving like a nut... And you don’t have a casino in your basement.”

“Well, I do own three slot machines in my garage. But that’s just because I like them. Like I enjoy my Greasegun. And my flame-thrower.”

“Flame-thrower?!”

"Yeah, for sentimental reasons. You know how I saved my men with a flame-thrower? — That's what I won my medal for, remember? I'll never use it, but when I hold it in my hands I remember how proud I was defending the country I love. Besides," Ben winked, "there's nothing better to light a cigar with."

Ted thought, *It's good to see Ben calm and happy.*

Ben remarked, serious again, "Nothing I've done has burdened anybody. Yet, I would have been in jail twenty times over if I didn't have my pardon. It's a matter of ethics not laws, actions not words, that make a person a good person."

"You know that Senator Shears really hates us."

"Well, I really hate him. I'll kick that SOB's ass," threatened Ben leaning forward in his seat.

"He's been saying that our pardons are illegal and he's trying to revoke them."

"He's a big HEAP."

"Yeah, from day one," noted Ted, "when he called to steal the Declaration and its glory from me. Now I hear he's trying to hold congressional hearings about us. Senator Dove, who's also on Shears' committee, is also publicly questioning our pardons and their impact on America."

Ted placed his pole into the nearest rod holder and slid his wallet out of his back pocket. His 3x5 bureaucratic scrapbook now contained only three things: cash, the picture of his dad and him, and his Freedom Card.

Ted slipped out his Freedom Card and read it, a ritual he did almost every day since he got it. On one side, the card was red, white and blue with gold trim and had the Presidential Seal. The back stated:

> In Contract with and by Executive Order of THE PRESIDENT OF THE UNITED STATES, the bearer of this card, THEODORE E. COMPASS, his heirs, agents, assigns, organizations, corporations, partners and/or associates are hereby granted total immunity and a blanket pardon for any and all past, present or future: taxes, regulations, malum prohibitum offenses and/or causes of action anywhere in the United States of America, its territories or its possessions.

Ted smiled, returned the card to his wallet and his wallet back into his pocket. He grabbed his fishing rod and cranked the line a few perfunctory turns. Suddenly, his rod tip jerked forward and the drag on his reel started singing.

"Got one!" exclaimed Ted.

A silvery-green bass jumped out of the water and danced in midair twenty feet ahead of the boat.

"Wow, it's a monster," encouraged Ben as he grabbed for the net.

Ted adjusted his grip to keep the line taut.

The large fish jumped again, then plunged for deeper water and weeds.

Ted held steady and continued to reel. The tactical fish almost tangled the line on some half-submerged timber, but Ted's experienced hands nonetheless maneuvered it to the boat.

"Watch out!" exclaimed Ben. "Don't lose it! Bring it in closer so that I can net it." Ben scooped up the catch and cheered, "I love it when the big ones *don't* get away!"

"You betcha!"

The heavy bigmouth flailed in the net.

Ted proudly opened their cooler as Ben put the big fish on ice.

Attempts By Their Legislatures

United States Senate
Ethics Committee

Subpoena to Appear

THEODORE E. COMPASS
ALICE ROSEN
BENJAMIN L. VERNON

Are hereby commanded to appear before the United States Senate Ethics Committee at a date and time to be set.

The Committee will be questioning you regarding your activities involving the Declaration of Independence.

You are hereby further commanded to bring any and all relevant documents, photographs or other records with you regarding the above. If you are disabled or need special accommodations, please contact your local representative.

Define Tyrant

"We now cut live to the congressional hearings in progress on the Presidential Special Privilege Grants of Immunity as headed by Senator Donald Shears, Chairman of the Ethics Committee..."

Members of the media and onlookers packed the hall like spectators at a wrestling match. Senator Shears sat pompously in the center of a raised podium flanked by Senator Dove and other senators. One wide, straight table spread below the Committee. Microphones were provided in front of each chair; however, there were only three chairs at the testimonial table: one for Ben, one for Ted, and one for Alice.

In a decade-old suit and tie, Ben leaned back subjectively in his chair; his hair was carefully parted and he was uncharacteristically clean-shaven. Ted, beside him in a navy blue, double-breasted suit, sat with both hands flat on the tabletop. Alice, comfortable in her sharp business attire, anchored the three with a natural poise and a full attaché at her side.

"....Keep in mind, Ladies and Gentlemen," summarized Shears waving a long silver pointer. "These charts represent only the tip of the iceberg of the problems created and forecasted to occur due to the President's recent grants of special privileges." The Senator was referring to graphs handed out in press release kits and projected on a large screen for all to see.

These graphs and charts illustrated:

- Forced Downsizing of Federal Government
- Lost Civil Service Jobs
- Federal Agency Reductions
- Economic Impact of Legalization of Marijuana and Ending of War on Drugs
- Impact of Professional Sexual Services
- Reduction of Federal and State Law Enforcement
- Downsizing of Judicial System
- Opinion Polls: American Reaction to Changes.

Shears continued, "The country is in chaos and our prized agencies — which are the envy and role model of governments around the world — are being rendered powerless. Some religious leaders are complaining that these recent changes will adversely affect America's morality. The American people are perplexed and confused. As head of the Senate Ethics Committee, I have chosen to respond to your pleas to examine this crisis."

With his pointer, the Senator motioned like a frustrated headmaster at Ted, who sat quietly at the center of the table looking up at the panel.

"It is our understanding that you held the United States Government hostage and refused to return property which was rightfully the government's, that property being the original Declaration of Independence. And, in exchange for the people of the United States of America getting back their document, you extorted the President of the United States of America into paying ransom to you in the form of Special Privilege Cards, which you and your cohorts have subsequently abused beyond anyone's imagination. Isn't this true, Mr. Compass?"

"First of all, Mr. Senator, I'd like to thank the Committee for allowing me the opportunity to address these issues you have inflamed and have been fanning in the media. It is absolutely true that I discovered, quite by accident, the original Declaration of Independence. However, Senator, in all your biased, self-serving statements, you conveniently forget to mention that *you* first called *me* to try to obtain the Declaration for your own political purposes."

"Don't twist my words. I've been trying all along only to get the people back their rightful property *and you know it*."

"No, Senator, you thought you could steal from me what was lawfully mine!"

"Mr. Compass, such outrageous allegations will not be tolerated by this committee." Shears ground his dentures and the gold buttons on his cuffs clicked against the podium.

"The truth will not be kept from the American people, Senator!"

Alice calmly cut in, "Senators, I would like to affirmatively state for the Committee that, first of all, the cards which the three of us possess, are not 'Privilege Cards' as you choose to call them, but rather 'Freedom Cards.' These cards simply restore to us the inherent rights which were proclaimed when the Declaration of Independence was signed, before our current government and laws grew out of control. I was simply given back what supposedly belongs to every American anyway. The purpose of our government is the protection of rights — not the channeling of rights, not the limiting of rights, and not the defining of inherent rights, which are self-evident and fundamental. It is a sad fact that citizens are once again forced to declare their rights."

"Our government, Ms. Rosen, is *for the people* and *by the people.*" The Senator sneered, "This government and these laws which you slam are wanted *by the people.* This legislature which enacts laws were voted in *by the people.* The system which you are so critical of and claim you want to restore created this great nation. Our sacred system should be preserved. You will not be allowed to abruptly change it by setting aside the *will of the people* and of our representative form of government."

Ted could not contain himself: "Our government has so suffocated in airtight vaults our founding documents — the Declaration of Independence, the Constitution and the Bill of Rights — that they can no longer breathe the air of freedom. It is only since my discovery that I have seen the truth. The system which elects our officials has been so manipulated and corrupted that our current government *of the people* is not trusted *by the people*." Ted rose from his chair and proclaimed: "I say: 'What country can preserve its liberties, if its rulers are not warned from time to time, that this people preserve the spirit of resistance?!'"

"It sounds to me as if you are advocating the violent overthrow of the United States Government."

"Actually, I'm quoting Thomas Jefferson. However, Senator. If you see me as a threat to your existence... you're right."

"Gentlemen," interjected Alice as she guided Ted back to his seat with a calming hand, "we're just looking for reasonable laws with a healthy respect for individual liberties. We are not anarchists. We are minarchists. We want to minimize government, not abolish it."

"Well, it still sounds like a conspiracy to overthrow the U.S. Government. Mr. Compass, you just stated that you are a threat to my existence!"

"Senator, I was speaking politically. I know what you are, and I will convey that message to any or all who wish to hear it."

"And what exactly am I, Mr. Compass?"

"You, sir, are a HEAP: A Hypocritical Elitist Authoritarian Politician. You can always spot a HEAP. They're the ones constantly proposing a ban or a tax. You HEAP on the laws, you HEAP on the taxes, you HEAP on the bureaucracies… You, sir, are a HEAP."

"Of shit!" punctuated Ben.

Gavels banged.

"Mr. Vernon, I demand you show deference to this Committee. And I need not remind you that this hearing is being broadcast live."

"I still have a First Amendment right enforceable by Presidential pardon to speak my mind," reminded Ben. "I also fought in Korea and thereby earned the right to call you and this hearing a HEAP of anything I damn well want."

"Senators," injected Alice, "we made a contractual agreement with the United States of America through its chief executive officer, the President, to secure the rights that we and our associates now enjoy. The return of freedom may temporarily disrupt America and require societal adjustments. However, it reminds me of something my mother would say whenever she put antiseptic on a cut and I complained about the sting: 'It stings because it's killing germs.'"

Shears wanted to end their forum and regroup. He gruffed, "Are there any more questions before we take a recess?"

Senator Earl Dove, who had been sitting back in contemplation, inched forward and sincerely asked, "Yes, I have one last question for Mr. Compass: Why did you three make this deal with the President and then embark on the course of conduct which brings you before us today?"

Ted was eagerly awaiting a question such as this.

Let the Facts Be Submitted

Ted removed a manuscript from his jacket, leaned into his microphone and declared:

When in the course of human events, it becomes necessary for one people to dissolve the political bands which have connected them with another, and to assume among the powers of the earth, the separate and equal station to which the laws of Nature and of Nature's God entitle them, a decent respect to the opinions of mankind requires that they should declare the causes which impel them to the separation.

I hold these truths to be self-evident, that all men are created equal, that they are endowed by their creator with certain unalienable rights, that among these are life, liberty, and the pursuit of happiness — That to secure these rights, governments are instituted among men, deriving their just powers from the consent of the governed, that whenever any form of government becomes destructive of these ends, it is the right of the people to alter or to abolish it, and to institute new government, laying its foundation on such principles, and organizing its powers in such form, as to them shall seem most likely to effect their safety and happiness. Prudence, indeed, will dictate that governments long established should not be changed for light and transient causes;

and accordingly all experience has shown, that mankind are more disposed to suffer, while evils are sufferable, than to right themselves by abolishing the forms to which they are accustomed. But when a long train of abuses and usurpations, pursuing invariably the same object, evinces a design to reduce them under absolute despotism, it is their right, it is their duty, to throw off such government, and to provide new guards for their future security. Such has been the patient sufferance of Modern Americans; and such is now the necessity which constrains them to alter their former systems of government. The history of the present government is a history of repeated injuries and usurpations, all having in direct object the establishment of absolute tyranny over the people. To prove this, let facts be submitted to a candid world.

They have passed malum prohibitum laws turning law-abiding citizens into criminals.

They have put schemes in place to disarm the people, in the pattern of registration, confiscation and forfeiture.

They have seized and forfeited personal and real properties with mock due process, judicial dishonesty and abuse of civil procedure.

They have violated the right to privacy and the right of the people to be secure in their persons, houses, papers and effects by conducting unreasonable searches and seizures, often without warrants and through tenuous legal arguments.

They have shifted the burden of proof through presumptions of law whereby individuals are guilty of offenses until they can prove themselves innocent.

They have promulgated an enormous, inconsistent and incomprehensible body of laws which no one person can fully comprehend, yet have ordained the burden of obeyance on the people to be fully accountable or be subjected to severe and disparate punishments and penalties.

They have imposed dictatorial bureaucracies to harass the people with ineffective and costly recourses for redress.

They have entrapped citizens, particularly those opposing authoritarianism, and put the full weight of judicial, executive, administrative and media systems against the people.

They have attacked, terrorized, maimed, and murdered citizens behind the guise of claiming to defend and protect children, the underprivileged, the environment, national interests and public safety.

They have excessively taxed and wastefully spent.

They have economically burdened the people by giving away enormous sums of foreign aid while our own infrastructure and national treasures deteriorate.

They have systematically discouraged American businesses through burdensome bureaucracies and illogical laws, regulations and policies, thereby putting American business at a severe disadvantage in foreign competition.

They have built an irrational and destructive civil tort system that discourages economic growth and is excessive and exploitive in its awarding of damages.

They have created a limited political system whereby two political parties are favored and funded; political campaign debate and true political discourse is curtailed; and the individual's vote has been rendered impotent.

They have imposed their agendas on a willing media and created state-run media to bolster their control and to block freedom of speech for those who oppose governmental policies.

They have denied and obstructed individuals and groups from exercising religious freedom.

They have endangered the family unit by establishing a dependent entitlement class through failed social programs and policies.

They have fostered racism by way of reverse discriminations, quota systems, and categorizations and compilations of racially based data; they have conspired against competence and individual achievement.

They have enforced involuntary servitude through registrations, drafts, antistrike laws, and mandatory pro-bono work requirements.

They have failed to protect our borders, tempting economic ruin and public health risks.

They have compiled a standing army to police the world for dubious political purposes of little or no national interest and have utilized these forces domestically against the people.

In every stage of these oppressions Americans have petitioned for redress in the most humble terms. Our repeated petitions have been answered only by repeated injury. A government, whose character is thus marked by every act which may define a tyrant, is unfit to be ruler of a free people.

I, therefore, a recipient of fundamental rights, appealing to the Supreme Judge of the World for the rectitude of our intentions, do, in the name, and by the authority of the good people to whom these rights have been extended, do solemnly publish and declare that all Americans are, and of right ought to be, free and independent. All Americans should be absolved from allegiance to hypocritical, elitist, authoritarian elements of the current government. All political connection between these corrupt elements and myself are and ought to be totally dissolved. For the support of this declaration, and of the Constitution of the United States, with a firm reliance on the protection of Divine Providence, I pledge my life, my fortune, and my sacred honor.

The room was silent.

Then, spontaneously, the audience — and even a handful of Committee members — rose and applauded.

Over the commotion Ben shouted to Ted, "I wish your dad could have heard you!"

Shears' gavel was lost in the uproar. He pressed into his microphone, shouting, "What's the meaning of this?! What are we going to have, everybody free?!"

The crowd ignored Shears, with the sole exception of Senator Dove. Dove turned to the disgruntled, red-faced senator beside him and posed, "Why not?"

Shears fell back into his seat, brooding. *Something has to be done regarding Compass, and soon.*

Human Events

The three friends stood in the shade of the hotel carport.

"We really shook 'em up. Didn't we, Ben?

"Like an earthquake, Ted. Like an earthquake."

"Actually, I can't believe how well this worked out. With Williamsburg so close, Washington was just a stop on the way."

"It's about time you two lovebirds finally got a chance to fly away together... Before I forget, I bought you each a little something for your visit."

"Aw, you didn't have to get us any—"

"We didn't get you anything for your fishing trip—"

"I saw some things I liked—" stressed Ben with a hand on each of their shoulders "—and I wanted you each to have something from me."

Ben reached into the back of his truck and handed Alice a poster tube and Ted a hatbox. Both presents were wrapped in red and blue paper with white bows.

Alice shook her tube. "Too light to be a flintlock."

"You bought me a hat?" Ted questioned.

"Open them when you get to Williamsburg."

The two thanked Ben and placed their presents on the backseat of Ted's mini-van.

Ben gave Alice a big kiss on the cheek and Ted his trademark bearhug. He waved goodbye till Ted and Alice pulled out of the parking lot.

After checking that his poles were stable in their bumper rack and that his trailer hitch was secure to his boat, the anxious fisherman sped off to get a few casts in before dark.

The Executioners

"You wanted to see me, boss?"

"Yes, I did, Carmine. Shut the door and come in." Ridge closed the door and paced to Shears' desk.

Shears looked up from some bills he was perusing. "As you know, Carmine, your decisive actions and inside information have saved us many times. As my future son-in-law, I'm damn proud of you. I've already done a lot for your career and offshore bank accounts. However, I'd like to provide a lot more for you than just money... You and I have a mutual problem. That problem being a certain Mr. Compass. He embarrassed you badly when he got the drop on you and Jack. Frankly, none of us are too fond of the man. He's undermining our plans and severely injuring our business concerns. However, I've got some good news. Right here in this envelope is a warrant for the arrest of one Mr. Theodore E. Compass."

Shears lifted a Manila envelope from the edge of his desk, drew out the sheet of paper within, and read:

> ...within the jurisdiction of this court did knowingly advocate and conspire for the violent overthrow of the government of the United States of America.

A rare smile overcame Ridge's face.

"What about the other two, sir?"

"I had to call in big favors just to obtain this one. The other two should fall in line after this warrant's been served." The Senator raised himself from his chair and put a hand on Ridge's shoulder. The agent detected a hint of bourbon on the Senator's breath. "Carmine, my boy, I want you to serve this warrant, and I want you to bring Mr. Compass to justice. But if by chance in the process, you or Agent Boots, attempting to do that — I want you to know —" The Senator moved in closer and spoke softer behind Ridge. "If Mr. Compass was to try to resist arrest or maybe to try to escape or to utilize the handgun that we all know he carries, I would hope and expect that you would *ex-e-cute* your duties faithfully because, if you were to *ex-e-cute* your duties, I see your career and finances advancing very, very quickly to our mutual advantage... Do you understand what I am saying to you?"

Ridge stared squarely forward at a portrait of Lyndon Johnson mounted behind Shears' desk. "Yes, sir. I absolutely do."

"Fine. Of course, we have a lot *in-vested* in this, so protect yourself and don't take any chances. I don't." The Senator pulled aside his tie and unbuttoned his shirt to expose his bulletproof vest. He tapped on it. "I also would suggest you keep this conference of ours between you and me."

Ridge turned to face the Senator. "Of course."

With this, the dispassionate agent pulled out his Sig-Sauer, racked the slide, and replaced the ready-to-fire pistol to his belt holster. "All points understood — perfectly."

Endowed By Their Creator

"There's something about a hotel room that always turns me on," cooed Alice while preening herself in the entrance mirror.

"I'm going to take unfair advantage of that, you know," bragged Ted who stood behind her.

"I expect my money's worth out of this hotel room," Alice continued, turning to face him.

"Well, you're gonna get your money's worth because, for the first time in my life since I was a kid, I feel totally uninhibited."

"I know exactly what you mean. With that hearing behind us, no clients to bother us, Freedom Cards in our wallets, and full bank accounts and growing portfolios, for once you and I can finally focus on what's important: loving each other." Alice pressed in closer. "How you handled yourself in front of that committee was moving and powerful."

Ted's arms wrapped around her waist and searched the depths of her eyes. "Without you, I would never feel the way I do right now. The obstacles to my emotions and battles for time have disappeared. All because of you. You figured out exactly what to do with the Declaration. You engineered the business deal of the century. You made the Declaration I found come to life. And, on top of all that, you're beautiful... What I am saying is: I love you."

"I love you, too."

Ted lowered his lips to hers with a passion and truth beyond even their first real kiss on their first date. Pecking across Alice's cheek to her ear, he surprised her with a whispered, "Will you marry me?"

Taking her hand in his, he placed his mother's engagement ring into her palm.

"Of course."

Ted had secretly resized the ring so it fit perfectly.

They kissed again.

Ted unbuttoned and lowered the silk blouse off Alice's arms and draped the garment over an easy-chair. He kissed her behind her ear and continued across her neck. Lowering to his knees, he nuzzled down the middle of her chest. He unbuttoned her slacks and helped her wriggle free. As he rose, he traced his fingers along the sides of her body. In one fluent motion, he scooped her up and placed her onto the quilted Colonial bed.

Ted relaxed beside her and sensually slid his arm under Alice's neck. "I would have gladly traded the Declaration for you."

She knew he meant it.

Cozy as the sheets of the Declaration tucked in their glass tube, two of the freest people in America celebrated their love. With unshackled minds, unshackled bodies and unshackled emotions, they united as one.

Bands Which Connected Them

They awoke to the sound of gunfire.

"I hear the reenactors on the Palace Green," informed Ted. "Drills and parades are scheduled all day."

Fingers raking Ted's chest, Alice ignored the echoes outside the window. "Honey, that was the most romantic night in my life."

"You've brought a lover out of me that I never knew existed."

"You know, what we did last night used to be illegal in five states," smiled Alice.

"I can't wait till tonight."

"Why wait?" Alice rolled on top of him.

Canons thundered in the distance.

The couple had visited Williamsburg a few months into their relationship. They vowed to return some day — in Colonial costume. Consequently, they had packed Revolutionary Period clothing; many articles they had bought on their first visit. By mid-morning, Alice had on a cream-colored market dress with flowered ribbons and fine, beige loafers. Ted wore a double-breasted shirt with ruffled cuffs, black britches, high white stockings and black leather shoes.

As Ted slipped into his fitted green jacket, he said, "It's always fun to put on this stuff."

Alice pointed to the table. "Hey, let's open up our gifts from Ben."

"Good idea."

Ted unwrapped his gift first.

"I don't believe it. Where did Ben find this?"

Ted lifted out a powdered, bleached wig. Alice laughed and carefully placed the wig over Ted's hair. A long white ponytail draped down the back of Ted's Colonial jacket.

"I don't think I'd recognize you if I didn't know you were wearing it."

Ted turned his profile to the left and cracked, "Would you recognize me on nickel?"

"Wow, you do resemble Thomas Jefferson!"

"That's probably why Ben bought it."

"Now, what could possibly be *my* present?"

Alice peeled back the endpapers of the wrapped tube and tilted out a lace parasol. She immediately popped it open and twirled it on her shoulder.

"I suppose this is Ben's way of showing me how much he appreciated the 'financial umbrella' I set up for him… It's lovely. Now, I'm a proper lady. Care for a stroll, Mr. Jefferson?"

Exposed

Sitting beside Ridge in an unmarked sedan, Boots queried, "How do you know they're out there?"

"Ran a credit check on all credit card uses by all three of them. They're there. At least Rosen is. You check their room. I'll start on the town."

I hope I run into that bastard first, thought Ridge.

Alice and Ted fit into the Glouster Street scene like time-travelers. As they meandered down the bricks, Ted sought conversations with the reenactors. Most conversations centered on how lovely the weather was and how wonderfully the town and nation were progressing.

On the corner of Glouster and Botetourt, a man also in fine period clothing approached Ted and started complaining in an Americanized British accent: "I think it is quite presumptuous of some upstart rabble-rousers to cause trouble for our King."

Ted laughed to himself, *I can't get away from this stuff.*

Ted countered, "Do not the King's policies of taxation annoy thee?"

The man grinned at receiving an in-character response and retorted, "The King provides us with protective services. Without the monarchy, who would govern us?"

“But, it’s rumored the King wants to disarm the Colonists.”

“Poppy-cock. He is only concerned with the best interests of the Colonies and the Empire. He would never dream of disarming his own loyal subjects. Besides, our armories are stocked.”

“What, sir, of our militia? Does it not consist of every able-bodied man? Shouldn’t each bear his own arms so it is at a moment’s ready to defend both himself and his countrymen?

“Yes, but their loyalties must be sworn to the King. If not, they should not be permitted to bear arms.”

“Sir, how shall we protect ourselves and our properties from unlawful search and seizures?”

“Unlawful? King George and his agents have immediate power to take at will. This, sir, *protects* public order. Though a well-dressed gentleman, you talk as if your sympathies lie with the rabble-rousers.”

“I and my wife more than sympathize. We consider ourselves *to be* rabble-rousers.”

“You are bordering on being labeled a traitor to fair Virginia.”

“Well, *pardon* me,” sarcasmed Ted.

“Good day, sir. Be careful where you tread.”

Ted and Alice ‘treaded’ onward, past the brick and board stores to the outdoor market at the end of the street. Alice wandered down to a hanging display of baskets while Ted scanned the tables of fruits, vegetables, ironwork, woodcarvings… Past faux-ivory trinkets and leather goods, Ted's eyes lighted on an exact reproduction of an Eighteenth Century deck of playing cards. He flipped the pack over in his hand; it even had a King's tax stamp on the back. Ted decided to buy the cards as a gift for Ben, who, he remembered, needed a deck of cards for his mountain retreat.

After paying for the item, he scanned for Alice who had wandered off to watch some street performers juggle and jest. Ted, instead, decided to join the growing crowd admiring a phalanx of militiamen drilling on the nearby Palace Green.

Twenty men dressed in Colonial military uniforms kaleidoscoped in and out of geometrical formations. An order would be barked and twenty rifles would thrust forward with precision or snap in unison to the soldiers' sides. The historic accuracy was hypnotic.

The militia marched downfield.

As much as Ted fit into the scene, he discerned an individual dramatically out of place across the Green wearing a black suit and tie. Ted shockingly recognized the man as his old antagonist, Agent Ridge. *Oh damn, what's that clown doing here? I wonder if his partner is around, too? This has got to relate to me somehow.*

Ridge felt the stare of the white-wigged man in the apple-green jacket. Like the focusing of a lens, it registered that this was the face he had been looking for all morning. The agent instinctively drew his weapon as the militia on the march returned and unintentionally blockaded Ted. Ridge bumped his way through the maneuvering columns.

He drew his gun! Ted alarmed as he bolted straight for the Governor's Palace.

As Ridge emerged from the soldiers, he tore after Ted and fired two shots in his direction.

He's trying to kill me! Ted dashed safely into the Palace.

A few spectators witnessed the chase, discriminated the handgun-fire from musket-fire, and started screaming.

One woman grabbed the nearest Minuteman and shouted, "That guy's trying to kill Thomas Jefferson!" to which the costumed man responded, "What do you want me to do about it, lady? We don't carry real bullets for these guns."

Agent Ridge followed Ted into the Palace with his gun pointing in front of him. In the 1700s, the Governor's Palace was purposefully decorated to impress and intimidate all who entered. Hundreds of swords, bayonets, flintlock muskets and pistols lined the paneling and ceiling in a hypnotic array. Ridge's eyes widened in awe of the symmetrical arrangements of arms everywhere. He was particularly mesmerized by the foyer ceiling, which suspended a circle of over sixty bayoneted flintlocks.

A flash of light reflected off a bright blade of steel.

Ridge gaped down in shock at his bloody, pruned wrist.

Lifeless on the marble tiles, his dismembered right hand still held his pistol.

From beside the door, Ted stepped before him, pressing his sword's tip to the agent's chest and commanding: "Freeze!" Ridge felt utterly powerless; he scanned the room for help but saw only silent, suspended weapons.

The agent's desperate mind recalled his back-up revolver secured to his ankle. Ted noticed Ridge's purposeful, downward motion.

"Stop!" shouted Ted as Ridge ignored his order.

In a pre-emptive strike, Ted thrust his full body weight on the sword, which easily sliced through Ridge's bulletproof vest. Ted continued to plunge until the hilt stopped the blade from going any further.

In a futile gesture, Ridge reached behind Ted's neck, grabbed the braid of Ted's wig, and gasped, "You've ruined everything."

"No, *you* have!" countered Ted with a twist of the sword. Ridge exhaled a final moan, collapsed to his knees and then slumped solidly facedown to the floor. A pool of blood spread from his body.

A touring party upstairs shouted: "Call the police! Call the police!" A number of costumed militiamen rushed in and seized Ted.

Abolishing the Free

The bass danced on top of the water like a ballerina. Ben fought the fish in to the strains of Johnny Cash's "I Walk the Line," which trebled thinly across the lake. The song ended as Ben netted his catch.

The station switched to a live, Presidential news conference: "Ladies and gentlemen, the President of the United States of America..."

"Members of the press and my fellow Americans, I have conferenced at length with several members of the Senate Ethics Committee. In brief, I and the Committee, and on behalf of the governors of the states, have determined that in the best interest of the people of the United States of America, the Presidential grants of immunity given to Alice Rosen, Benjamin Vernon and Theodore Compass last October are, hereby, revoked... I'm sure there are questions..."

There was a moment of silence and then a storm of reporters apparently vied for the President's attention.

"Mr. President, wasn't the pardon a written and signed contract. Won't you now have to give the original Declaration of Independence back."

"If a President can pardon, he can take it away. The original Declaration of Independence belongs to the American people and to history, not just to any one man."

"Mr. President, are you taking this action because of the recent death of the FBI agent who was allegedly murdered by pardoned Theodore Compass two days ago."

"Mr. Compass' pardon did not cover violent crimes. That incident did weigh into our decision, of course, but mostly it was the influence of Senator Shears who finally persuaded me that this is the right thing for America. Unfortunately, our advisors did not properly explain to me all the implications of granting such immunities. Instead, I had the country's best interests at heart in wanting to obtain our sacred and original Declaration of Independence."

"Where is Mr. Compass now?"

"As far as my knowledge, he's being held in a federal facility just outside Washington."

"On what charges?"

"I believe the charges are officially 'murder of a federal agent and conspiracy to overthrow the United States Government,' but I cannot comment any further on the case."

"Does this mean that the recent freedoms and open markets many Americans are starting to experience will again be taken away?"

"What it means is that we have restored law and order and that public safety is our first concern. Our government can once more take care of the American people."

"Mr. President, did Senator Shears threaten or pressure you with regard to the Vatican allegations if you did not revoke these pardons?"

"I was never threatened with a such a statement, though as I've mentioned, the legality of these pardons has been questioned. This news conference is to set the record free of doubts...."

Shears... That damn bastard! Ben angrily yanked the motor's pullcord and sped full-throttle straight for shore.

Seeing behind the President's statements, Ben vowed: *Shears will not get away with this!*

A Candid World

"Good evening, America, Max Crier here with another edition of *Town Crier*. We have an exclusive tonight in our series of programs dedicated to examining the ongoing ramifications of the revoked Presidential pardons signed in exchange for the original Declaration of Independence. With us tonight is Alice Rosen, one of 'The Freedom Three' whose Presidential pardons have today been nullified. She is also the fiancée of Theodore Compass, who is currently incarcerated on charges of murder of a federal agent and of conspiracy to overthrow the United States Government. Ms. Rosen is here to answer questions regarding the recent actions taken by the President of the United States of America at the behest of Senator Shears and the Senate Ethics Committee.

"But first, we have sent our Crier Fire Team out to the streets for public opinion." The show switched to a previously recorded, man-on-the-street report. A woman on a bus-stop bench stated how glad she was that the pardons were revoked and that she wanted to see police enforcement of the old laws. A muscular man straddling a bicycle stated that he doesn't want the old laws back and prefers the freedom to choose for himself. A blonde woman with reading glasses sitting on the steps to a grammar school said that she had mixed feeling about it; her stocks were doing well, but she did not like that prostitution was legal. From the open window of his car, a man with a heavy Eastern European accent stressed how he loved the new liberties. A petite gray-haired man in a suit exclaimed, "It's been great for business."

"Max," voiced the reporter, "these are typical of the varied responses I've received all day today. Polls show that approximately one third of the people support Ms. Rosen and her actions, about a third don't, and about a third of the public is neutral… Lynn Chen reporting from Baltimore. Now, back to you, Max."

"Alice Rosen, thank you for being on our program."

The camera pulled out to show Alice and Crier at an interview desk.

Crier continued, "What do you think about the mixed support that you have from the people?"

"It's ironic, Max. During the American Revolution also: about a third of Americans supported the rebels, about a third supported the Tories, and about a third were neutral."

"So I guess things haven't changed much?"

"Oh, no, things have changed a lot. The men who founded this country obviously would not have stood idly by in the face of the destruction of American liberties and they would surely not have stood for the tyranny of the majority taking away individual freedoms."

"What 'tyranny of the majority?'"

"I am referring to individuals being crushed by the will of the majority. Our founding fathers specifically put in place checks and balances to allow for personal, yet perhaps unpopular, beliefs and actions to exist. Our fundamental rights were never to be determined by the latest opinion poll."

"Ms. Rosen, how do you feel about your pardons being revoked?"

"Max, that was clearly a breech of contract. It sends a clear message regarding the trustworthiness of the U.S. Government to stand by an agreement. Now, I know how the American Indians must have felt and why they let Custer have it at Little Big Horn. We are already seeking redress in the courts; however, the entire system is slanted against us, now more than ever because we, for several months, didn't acknowledge it."

"What does all this mean?"

"It means the time has come for Americans to make a choice as to whether they want more government or less government, whether they want to stand for the collective or for the individual."

"Yes, this comports with our investigation which shows that there are a lot of dissatisfied people out there. They are quite upset, as you note, that such an action by the President could be unilaterally taken after a formal deal has been agreed to by and on behalf of the United States of America."

“Apparently, I’ve garnered lots of support. Deregulation was starting to help a lot of people and was poised to help a lot more. For the short time I had freedom restored, businesses and citizens had renewed energies and positive outlooks.”

“There’s been talk of underground militias and resistance movements on the rise. Are you associated with or have you been contacted by any such organizations?”

“No, I do not personally know of any. What I do know is that drug companies were able to quickly introduce experimental, life-saving drugs, that the telephone company and Internet providers never offered better services, that individuals could lawfully protect themselves against criminals who formerly preyed on them without fear, that drug dealers and pimps were going out of business, that organized crime was on the run, that bureaucratic red-tape was at the end of its roll, and that freedom of speech required no protection.”

“Was this too much too soon for the American people?”

“No, it was too little and almost too late. But now, Americans have again tasted freedom. It is not going to be easy to return to our old stifled and repressed lives. Since the President’s breech of contract, the stock markets are going down. There have been threats of riots and violence; the President has had to put the National Guard on alert. People fear economic depression and now that is being compounded with an actual resumption of our former police state.”

“What if the Congress takes action?” posed Crier.

“Well, so far, all our legislature has ever done is curtail our freedoms with new law after new law. I would love to see repeal. But, Max, it is no wonder people are so frustrated. Over years and years, their release valves had been slowly stripped away. A person should be able to enjoy a smoke, or to download with a drink on his porch, or to play music in the park, or to hunt or to fish, or to have sex with any consenting adult he or she chooses, or to jog safely through the streets. You may call some of these activities vices; I call them freedoms. Man should not to be taxed to death, suffocated by paperwork or strangled by red tape.

“Citizens should be able speak their minds without fear of political correctness. Unfortunately, the people are too afraid to offend or to be sued or to be targeted by an agency. No wonder we harbor such aggressions and low self-esteems. No wonder road rage exists. All our ways to free our minds and bodies have been limited, snubbed, outlawed or labeled “verboten” under the guises of good laws, good manners, or ‘good for you.’ Americans are sick of the do-gooders who think they know what’s best for everyone and who want their morality enforced by law. I believe people should have total choice in their lives. I’m not telling anyone what choices to make and I don’t want anyone telling me.”

"What efforts are you making to get your fiancé out of jail?" Max queried.

"Ted acted purely out of self defense. Witnesses report that the government agent was trying to kill my unarmed fiancé. Furthermore, Ted never advocated the violent overthrow of this government. In fact, he totally embraces America's Constitution and simply read to the Senate an updated version of the Declaration of Independence. Apparently Senator Shears only cares about the document and not what it stands for. The same can be said for Shears' view of the Constitution and for the Bill of Rights."

"Are you and your fiancé seeking the return of the original Declaration now that your pardons have been revoked?"

"No. In sharp contrast with Senator Shears, our primary concern has always been what the Declaration of Independence represents and not the document itself… I have scheduled a rally in support of Ted for seven o'clock this Friday in front of the federal penitentiary where he is being detained. We are holding a candlelight vigil in support of Ted's release."

"Well, we agreed to let you plug your vigil in exchange for your appearance on our show. We hope that you are successful in peacefully resolving these issues... Next up, we have a university professor to explain political change and its influence on society…."

Absolute Despotism

"Come in, Jack. Come in," Shears greeted Boots while sweeping shut the door behind him. "It's a dirty shame about what happened to Carmine."

"Yes, it is," stonily agreed Boots. "We never should have separated to search for Compass."

"Well, try not to agonize over it. I understand how you feel. As you know, Carmine was going to marry my daughter Clipper. Unfortunately, we can't change the past."

"Carmine and I were friends since we were kids," informed Boots. "We fought together in Central America. We vowed we'd always cover each other's ass and payback our enemies."

"Good! You'll get your chance to do just that... I know you're very upset about this, but he was just following orders."

"Orders?"

"That's right. He was assigned to neutralize Compass."

"Why didn't you have me in on it? I could have saved him."

"I wanted to maintain plausible deniability for you."

"The hell with me!" raged Boots. "You cost my buddy his life."

Shears rested a heavy hand on Boots' shoulder. "Jack, we're all doing the best we can to combat this threat to our interests. However, now we know the seriousness of what we're up against."

Shears guided his agent into an armchair. Boots sat stiffly as Shears paced behind him.

"I've just become privy to some disturbing information," Shears monotoned. "My colleague, Senator Dove, confidentially revealed to me that he is garnering bi-partisan support to put forward legislation to repeal upwards of twenty percent of, how he put it, 'unnecessary, outdated and restrictive laws on the books.' He told me that 'perhaps, after 200 years, it is time to clean house' and that this legislation is just the beginning, and that he intends to hold televised 'town meetings' within the month to promote his bi-partisan 'freedom' plans."

Shears sat in the chair opposite Boots and continued, "We've got to clip this bird's wings, and his elimination has been approved by our most powerful friends. Here's what I'm ordering you to do:

"Our intelligence has revealed that Benjamin Vernon will be away from his home for at least the next few days. You need to black bag him, sneak into his house and get his flame-thrower. However, it is Senator Dove who is actually your clay pigeon... Every Tuesday morning when Dove is in his hometown, he stops at his family-owned gas station accompanied only by his limo driver. His driver is also an armed bodyguard. It has been decided that this is our best opportunity to roast Dove and incinerate his plans."

The agent watched as Shears' wrinkled face shook with hatred down to his jowls. Boots staccatoed in disbelief, "You want me to assassinate a U.S. Senator? Do you know how much heat will be on me for this?"

"If done right, Vernon will burn. Anyway, I've already got enough dirt on you to bury you... I don't want it to come to this... You really don't have a choice in the matter. Just obey orders."

"I don't like being threatened, *Don.*"

If you do this properly, Dove will be out of the way and our dear Mr. Vernon will be in a 'HEAP of shit' himself. Public sentiment will be completely against Vernon, Compass and Rosen. Along with the President's recent revocations, this should put an end to this 'freedom' problem once and for all."

Shears' cheeks and nose flushed red. "You're a smart guy, Jack. Don't blow it."

For Taking Away Our Charters

A growing crowd dressed in colorful clothing gathered as participants in Tri-County's 22nd Annual Medieval Renaissance Faire. In contrast to the checkered jesters, loud peasants and gleaming armored knights, a man in a simple brown monk's robe wrapped with a plain hemp belt worked his way through the small groups of merrymakers. Only the lit tip of a Cohiba poked out of the oversized hood shrouding his face.

Surveying the layout of the arena, the monk meandered his way to the rear of the crowd. In front of his oversized cloak, he proudly clasped a Barnett crossbow.

A burly, armored man with a goatee and a sponge mace blocked the monk and commented: "Enjoying the fair, Friar?"

"Aye," answered the startled man.

"You know the Pope has outlawed them."

"Cigars?"

"No, the Satanic weapon in your hands whose bolts of death penetrate armor. The Pope has banned crossbows for they wield too much power against the King's knights, such as myself. But I can see you are no threat... Who are you supposed to be? Some kind of moral crusader?"

"Yes, for freedom."

"Best fortunes to you, Father, in all your missions."

The saintly man bowed and paced away as if suddenly remembering a vow of silence. What was not visible to the curious knight was that the monk's robe hid a quiver of razor-headed bolts with poison payloads. Rubber sacks full of poison fit around each crossbow bolt directly behind each broadhead; if a bolt were to enter a target, the sacks would roll back and discharge a curare-like poison.

A man dressed as a court jester jingled his way across the fair's soundstage to a microphone: "You may have noticed this year's latest addition to the fair grounds. I'm standing on it!" The jester stomped on the platform. "Our new stage was finished just last week as part of a matching grant through the State Humanities Council. Also, the U.S. Senate donated these beautiful, patriotic flags draped around our stage and podium. In honor of our new stage, I'd like to be the first to call it by its official name. For the man who made it all possible: The Senator Donald Shears Renaissance Stage! And, we're proud to have with us today, United States Senator Donald Shears himself, who would like to say a few words to his constituency in light of this dedication."

The crossbow-wielding monk stood between two apple trees at the rear of the crowd, about thirty-five yards from the stage. He dropped and stomped on his half-finished cigar. With a heft, the monk lifted himself into the tree nearest him and perched himself on a thick limb.

The Senator was shaking hands and thanking the bearded jester on stage as the friar firmly secured himself in a crux of the apple tree. The robed man cocked the crossbow and set a bolt into the weapon's furrow.

Through loudspeakers the Senator's voice projected across the small field with a faint squeaky feedback: "Lords'n ladies, it's truly a glorious day for a fair!"

Shears waited for the cheers to fade.

"There's been a lot of talk about freedom lately and about the roles elected officials play in your lives. As your humble servant, I hope you plainly recognize how much I love freedom. But, in order to be free, a nation must exercise control and discipline, and that is what I and many of my colleagues in Congress have set out to do as your representatives. George Washington and Thomas Jefferson and Benjamin Franklin would be proud of the America we have become.

"We pass laws to let you live free. Our laws *are* freedom!

"I hear your complaints about high taxes, but as you know, more taxes make you freer by empowering the government to spend freely more money to help you. Every law that we pass is a tribute to the viability of the Constitution and a penny in the bank for liberty!"

The Senator paused for effect. Delayed, the crowd realized they were supposed to clap and lightheartedly did so.

"I hear your complaints about crime. However, you all know my slogan — *Society is everyone but yourself.* Criminals are not responsible for crime. Society is responsible for crime because only those members of society who do not commit crime can be held responsible. This is why it is your responsibility as an American to fight crime by doing what is best for society.

"I understand you can't go out safely, so I enacted laws to ban guns and ammunition. Congress only 'bans' things to make you free, free to enjoy your lives. For example, we know that you hate drug dealers, so we've enacted super-tough laws banning drugs.

"Your congressmen and senators are here to help. We know that you want to end prostitution, so we've specifically passed laws to stop men from wanting to have sex with prostitutes.

"We don't want individuals losing their incomes to unofficial gambling operations, so we passed legislation prohibiting it. This ensures that only the right kind of people own and run gambling operations.

"People commit crimes with cars, and in houses, and with money… When we catch them, we make them give their instruments of crime to our law enforcement agencies to use or to sell as they see fit. This costs you nothing and helps us to protect your property.

"You've demanded fair housing. You deserve fair housing. So that you can afford living quarters cheaply, we've passed rent-control legislation. Of course, who knows better what an apartment should rent for than the government?

"We recognize the inability of minorities to make it on their own, so we have created special programs to help them, too.

"I love freedom. However, your representatives have shown compassion, which is much more important than freedom. We have shown that having good intentions is more important than freedom. Striving for a perfect world is exceedingly more important than——"

WHAP!

Suddenly, the shaft of a crossbow bolt was sticking out the center of Senator Shears' chest. The bolt effortlessly penetrated his vest and delivered its poison payload.

The crowd screamed in a mix of horror and shock.

The bolt quivered slightly. Frothy blood poured from the Senator's mouth as he slumped with a thud onto his microphone. A dark stream ran down the flag wrapped around the front of the podium and dripped off the platform. Shears' assistants and a variety of Medieval characters ran to his side as a maroon puddle coagulated on the stump of a tree cut to make room for the stage.

The friar shimmied his way down the trunk. As his feet touched the ground, he swung around. In front of him stood a broad-shouldered, dark-skinned police officer staring down at him.

The monk immediately dropped his crossbow and put up his hands —waiting for an opportunity to draw for his concealed pistol and surprise the officer.

However, the policeman picked up the crossbow and pushed it back at him. "My last name's Jefferson, and I know what it means. I hated that corrupt bastard, too. Get the hell out of here."

The shocked monk didn't stick around to discuss politics with the officer. Instead, he ran to his dark sedan and immediately drove away.

After hurriedly dialing on his cell phone, the monk pulled down his hood to speak. He reported:

> This is Agent Jonathan Boots. I want an APB put out on one Benjamin L. Vernon, who I just observed shooting United States Senator Donald Shears with a crossbow. I have recovered his crossbow weapon, however Mr. Vernon should still be considered armed and dangerous. He was last seen wearing a brown monk's costume at Tri-County's Renaissance Faire driving a red Blazer. License plate...

As he waited for the Bureau's confirmation, he shook his head disbelievingly—

> *He gave me back the crossbow and let me go!*
>
> *What the hell is this country coming to?*

To Secure These Rights

Candles in waxpaper cups flickered in the evening air outside the federal penitentiary. Banners and picket boards supported Ted's cause, demanding his release:

FREEDOM FOR THE FREEDOM MAN.

FREE TED! HE FREED U S!

OUR COMPASS IS TRUE!

Hundreds of people greeted each other as if they each knew one another — with the exception of one agent with a mission. Boots stood out from the crowd like an X on a page of Os.

Even the Agent noticed how the news of Shears' assassination was causing a rebellious energy in the crowd. *These people are actually glad to hear of Shears' demise.*

Wearing tinted glasses and a low-brimmed hat, Ben Vernon inconspicuously worked his way through the ralliers. Alice was shuffling notecards and pacing along the prison fenceline when Ben approached her.

"Ben!" she gasped in recognition, then hurried: "I'm so happy to see you again! But it's all over the news that you assassinated Senator

Shears. You're in danger of being caught and killed here. Ridge tried to murder Ted. He shot at him first and without warning. It was a set-up, Ben. They'll try to kill you, too. I'm sure. Especially with Shears dead."

"I didn't kill our beloved Senator. Even though he is the man who extorted the President, set up Ted, took away our freedom, and stands for everything I fought against in the war."

Alice looked at him with a raised eyebrow. "Then who did?"

"I don't know, but my crossbow was stolen out of my house and I've been framed. I know I'm in danger, but I'm protecting myself. I'm not taking any chances." Ben patted the side of his jacket. "Good luck on your speech. Just get our Teddyboy outta there. Don't worry about me."

Boots scanned the crowd and discerned that it was in fact Mr. Vernon chatting with Ms. Rosen. He knew Ben would be armed and that he had to solidly get the drop on him. *Dead men tell no tales. With that old coot eliminated, there will be no alibis and no basis to question the identity of Shears' assassin... This will work even better than bulldozing a crime scene.*

Withdrawing his Sig-Sauer, the agent slithered up beside Ben.

Pressing the barrel into Ben's ribs, he whispered, "You're a dead man."

Ben spun around, knocking Boots' gun with one hand while drawing out his own cocked and locked .45 with his other.

Boots saw the advancing gleam of steel in the candle lights.

The two guns discharged simultaneously.

Both men fell backwards.

Damn, he was fast! thought Boots as blood and balance drained out of his body.

Ben continued to empty his gun into Boots as they fell. One round caught the agent in the eye, blowing out the back of his head.

Running from the fence, Alice was quickly at Ben's side. Blood pumped out of his abdomen and onto the grass. "Ben, can you hear me? Stay awake. Talk to me!"

She lifted his bloody shirt and attempted to apply direct pressure to his wound. Though he looked right at her, Ben's eyes glazed.

He gasped, "Americans will have freedom returned to them…"

Ben passed out and the ground started shaking.

Alice was scared and confused. She looked up and saw three National Guard tanks driving directly towards her through the dispersing crowd.

Surprisingly though, the tanks curved around Alice and Ben and headed on toward the prison gates and walls. The lead tank crashed down a section of wall like a domino then rammed a hole where the front door of the prison once stood.

The excited mob poured in around Ben and Alice and behind the advancing tanks.

Ought To Be Free

There was a small explosion, followed by a larger explosion.

The entrance to Ted's cell glided open and a man in a military uniform appeared.

"Ted Compass?"

"Yes."

"Come on. We're getting you out of here."

Ted had been using his jail time to journal and reflect on his experiences since he bought the Revolutionary flintlock. He grabbed his notebooks off the concrete table and followed the soldier out the door, no questions asked.

Other inmates followed.

Pistol and sub-machinegun fire clapped and reported down the spartan corridors, however Ted sensed that a skilled and trustworthy man was guiding him.

New Guards

It was a chaotic scene outside the penitentiary. People were running in all directions through dusky drifts of smoke. Gunfire still popped from the prison and tanks still vibrated the ground.

After stepping over a downed fence beside the soldier who freed him, Ted rushed to Alice who faithfully knelt beside their dying friend. Comforting an arm around her shoulder, he gasped, "What happened to Ben?"

Continuing to press Ben's torso, Alice's hands were awash with blood. She motioned with tear-filled eyes at the nearby riddled corpse of Agent Boots.

"Medic! Medic!" A nearby soldier windmilled his arms towards the scene.

The Guardsman who had broken into Ted's jail cell remained at Ted's side. The officer put out his hand and informed, "I'm Lieutenant Allen, commander in the Grandsons of Liberty. These Guardsmen are enraged about America's loss of freedom. Your actions inspired us. We know you are innocent. Come with us. We'll take you to safety…"

Ted pried the gun out of Ben's hand.

A breathless recruit ran up to Lieutenant Allen. "Immediate perimeter secure, sir. Now what?"

Ted gave a hard look at Ben's .45 and answered for the Lieutenant:

"We all know what follows a Declaration."